# Flaming Hearts

*Flaming Hearts*

BEYOND REALITY
BOOK 2

## By Susan Stoker

This book is a work of fiction. Names, characters, places, and incidents are products of the author's imagination or are fictitiously. Any resemblance to actual events or locales or persons living or dead is entirely coincidental.

Copyright © 2014 by Susan Stoker

No part of this work may be used, stored, reproduced or transmitted without written permission from the publisher except for brief quotations for review purposes as permitted by law.

This book contains material protected under International and Federal Copyright Laws and Treaties. Any unauthorized reprint or use of this material is prohibited. No part of this book may be reproduced or transmitted in any form or by any means, electronic or mechanical, including photocopying, recording, or by any information storage and retrieval system without express written permission from the author.

Cover Design by Chris Mackey, AURA Design Group

Manufactured in the United States

ALL RIGHTS RESERVED

# Table of Contents

| | |
|---|---|
| Chapter One | 1 |
| Chapter Two | 12 |
| Chapter Three | 19 |
| Chapter Four | 27 |
| Chapter Five | 38 |
| Chapter Six | 70 |
| Chapter Seven | 79 |
| Chapter Eight | 104 |
| Chapter Nine | 114 |
| Chapter Ten | 140 |
| Chapter Eleven | 156 |
| Chapter Twelve | 164 |
| Chapter Thirteen | 174 |
| Chapter Fourteen | 182 |
| Chapter Fifteen | 218 |
| Epilogue | 225 |
| Discover other titles | 232 |
| Connect with Susan Online | 234 |
| About the Author | 235 |

## Chapter One

REBECCA WAS EXCITED. She couldn't believe it was finally time for her reality show to start! Becky was a reality show junkie. She'd started watching reality shows when she was a little girl and couldn't believe she was finally going to be on one.

Becky used to watch with her mom when she was sick. It was a great way to get away from the reality of the disease that was taking her mom's life away one day at a time. Her mom refused to go into hospice care and wanted to die at home. So Becky did as she wished. She had no siblings, and her dad had died a long time ago. It was just her and her mom.

They'd laughed at the contestants, at their scheming and conniving ways, but loved every minute of the shows. They weren't particular as to what kind of reality shows they'd watch. Love matches, cop shows, extreme survival shows, teenagers getting pregnant…it didn't matter. What mattered was the time they spent together.

Becky applied to every show she could with her mom's help. They had a blast printing off the forms and finding the best way to market Becky. Neither figured she'd ever get chosen. After all, millions of people probably applied to be on the shows, but it was fun nevertheless.

They'd also had a long conversation about the kinds of women who were typically chosen to be on reality shows. Actresses, models, former beauty pageant queens…it was really quite nauseating. Very rarely did they see any women on the shows who were considered "normal."

Becky's mom died before knowing she'd been chosen to be on a show. It was bittersweet. She admitted to herself that she was excited to be chosen, but was also sad because Becky knew her mom would never see her on TV.

The show she'd been chosen to be on was a bachelorette type of show. She wasn't too fond of most of the reality shows that were currently running, but Becky figured it might be worth giving it a try. Thank goodness she wasn't chosen for one of the survivalist-type shows. She shuddered. She knew she'd never make it even one day on one of those, not that she'd ever even apply for one. She hated bugs, hated to be cold, or hot, and wasn't an outdoorsy type of person, except for the occasional hike. She knew the show she'd be on would be different from what was airing now, but she had no idea how.

All she knew was that she'd get to choose from a posse of men! Now *that* was exciting. Her love life had suffered over the last few months because of taking care of her mom, but she wouldn't have had it any other way.

The last reality love-type show she'd watched was one that had been filmed in Australia. The man on that show had been very good looking. Becky had applied for that show, but obviously wasn't chosen. The producer of that show was also producing the one she'd be on. Becky loved the twists and turns of the Australian production, and hoped some fun things were going to happen in her show as well. Of course, watching people run after pigs and shovel manure was probably a lot more fun to watch than it was to actually do in person. Oh well. She was excited anyway.

Becky wasn't exactly sure how she'd gotten chosen for this show. She knew she wasn't a typical bachelorette. She was a bit older than a lot of the women she'd seen on TV. She wasn't over the hill yet, hell she was only 32, but she also wasn't in her early twenties either. She wasn't an actress or a model. She'd never been on television before. She was just…Becky.

She had a normal job. She wasn't an executive and she didn't own her own business. She worked for an insurance company as an underwriter. Her job was to accept applications as they came in and look them over to make sure that whatever the person wanted insured was eligible. Houses had to be in good condition, Becky had to check the claim history to make sure it wasn't excessive and other things related to the application. She also took phone calls from agents and policyholders to discuss the policies and answered any questions they had. The worst was when the policy was cancelled. No one was happy and they usually took it out on her, which wasn't fun at all. All in all, her job was perfectly normal and actually quite boring. But it paid the bills.

Becky was flattered Eddie and the other producers had chosen *her* to be the bachelorette on their show. She'd never known any of the other women on the dating shows she'd watched to have a normal job as she had.

Apparently the producers had noticed her application for the Australian show and decided she'd be a perfect bachelorette for their new reality show. Becky knew she was heavier than the women that had been showcased before. However, she'd read that Alex, the bachelor in Australia, in the end had chosen a woman—she couldn't remember her name—that wasn't model thin either. Maybe there was hope for her yet! Becky knew she wasn't obese by any stretch, but she also wasn't bikini material either. She'd rather go hiking than clubbing, but on the other hand she'd rather hang out watching TV than go shopping. And she'd rather do just about anything other than put on a fancy dress and makeup! But Becky had put her best face forward in the application and through subsequent interviews, and apparently she'd passed the psychological tests. Now she was on her way to Arizona to participate on the show.

She had no idea what would come out of the experience. Would she fall in love and get married? Would she become famous? Would she hate the entire experience and become a bitter old woman? There was no telling what would happen. That was part of the excitement.

She'd been given the five star treatment throughout her travel to Arizona. They flew her first class and she'd been driven to the huge mansion she'd be staying at by a limousine, complete with a stern faced driver. She met the host of the show and he seemed nice enough. She was a bit giddy because the host was the same as the Australian show, Robert. It was like meeting a movie star!

She'd be at the house for two months while they filmed. Eight weeks didn't seem long enough to be able to meet a man and fall in love, but she knew being on these shows really accelerated the dating process because it was so intense. She wasn't allowed to talk to anyone from her "real world," of course, unless there was an emergency, and she wasn't allowed to watch television at all. There wasn't really anyone who she'd miss. Oh, she had friends, but they were mostly work acquaintances. She had some people from the animal shelter she volunteered at that she might miss, but again, they were more work acquaintances than true friends.

Becky knew she'd miss her mom, though. They'd both talked about what would happen if she was ever chosen to be on a show and she'd miss being able to talk and gossip with her mom when she got home in eight weeks. The thought of actually sitting down and watching the show when it aired without her mom was also very hard to imagine.

Becky was able to take a leave of absence from the insurance company and luckily she had a good boss who'd let her come back after the show was over. She didn't have leave time saved up to cover the entire eight weeks, but Human Resources was allowing her to take leave-without-pay to cover the rest of the time that she didn't have the time for. It was very generous of them actually.

Her coworkers had thrown a huge party for her on her last day of work. They'd all teased her about becoming rich and famous and forgetting all about them. Becky had laughed. It wasn't as if being an underwriter was anyone's dream job. She knew they'd all leave in a heartbeat if they could. But she was touched that everyone wished her well, especially considering they'd have to take up her slack on the job since she wouldn't be there.

Overall, she was ready. She couldn't wait to meet the men on the show. She figured if she fell in love great, but if not, at least it'd be an experience to remember!

JONATHAN STOOD WITH the other camera operators listening to instructions given to them by Eddie, the producer of the reality show. Jonathan had sort of fallen into the whole camera operator gig and was finding that it really wasn't his thing, but he'd agreed to work on two last jobs, this one and one last show in Alaska. He was thrilled this show was filming in Arizona because he'd been working in Los Angeles for the past four years and he missed his brother and the rest of his close-knit family. They were a bit crazy, but he wouldn't change anything about them.

When he was done with his camera operator contract, his brother, Dean, said he could come home and work with him. Jonathan was thrilled. Dean had worked his butt off and finally had a job he loved. He was a security expert and got called to consult all over the country on both big and small cases. He'd visit a business or home and recommend what security was needed based on the client's needs. He'd consulted for huge corporations down to small seven hundred square foot homes.

Jonathan was also not surprised when he'd heard Dean would take cases pro-bono for women who were trying to protect themselves from stalkers or violent ex's. Jonathan couldn't wait to make a difference in someone's life as he knew Dean was. Filming people trying to become famous, if only for their five minutes of fame, wasn't how he wanted to be remembered. He couldn't wait to work with his brother professionally.

Jonathan was in his mid-thirties and wasn't ashamed about wanting to be closer to home. His family had always been close. He missed Dean. Jonathan smiled when he thought about his older brother. Neither of them had ever been married. Jonathan had come close once, but it didn't work out. Dean was a strong man. Someone who knew what he wanted and didn't put up with any crap from anyone, male or female. Jonathan knew most people thought Dean was way too intense. He was an alpha male to the nth degree. Jonathan loved that about his brother. When he was little, Dean not only protected Jonathan from bullies who thought he should be into sports rather than art and photography, but Dean also protected everyone else too.

There was one day Jonathan remembered when their mom had gotten a call from the local police chief and demanded they bring Dean into the station. The whole family went down to the station with Dean and heard the police chief lambast him for beating up the local high school football hero.

Their dad requested Dean explain what was going on. Jonathan would never forget his brother standing in the small interrogation room, defiant even at fifteen years old, and calmly explaining how he'd walked around the corner of the high school and seen the boy hitting his girlfriend. He'd stepped in and beat the crap out of the boy in retaliation. He'd seen someone in need and stepped in and did what was necessary. He hadn't cared who the boy was. It didn't matter he was a football hero and one of the most popular guys at the school…and older than him to boot. He did what was right. Period.

Jonathan knew Dean would do anything for him too. Family meant a lot to them. He'd missed that. He missed the feeling of belonging. While he still belonged to his family, it was hard to connect with them when he was in Los Angeles and they were all back in Arizona.

Jonathan turned his attention back to Eddie as he spelled out the duties of the camera operators for the shoot. They'd rotate jobs throughout the day and throughout the show. Eddie felt it wasn't good for one camera operator to get too close to any of the contestants, and vice versa. When Jonathan tried to bring up the fact that sometimes if the contestants were more comfortable with the camera operator they seemed to open up more and be more themselves, Eddie didn't want to listen.

Jonathan knew this was going be a tough shoot. Eddie seemed to have an agenda and he was acting pretty sneaky. He knew Eddie had been in charge of the reality show that had just ended in Australia and apparently made a ton of money for the network. He couldn't remember all the details, but thought he remembered reading something about a ton of twists and turns throughout the show. Why anyone would want to be on a reality show was beyond his comprehension. Jonathan mentally shrugged and told himself it was a job and it was money, and he really didn't care what went on with the spoiled contestants…as long as he was paid, he didn't care.

BECKY TOOK A deep breath and tried to calm herself. She'd just come from a meeting with the producer and couldn't believe what she'd gotten herself into. She was so excited to have been chosen for the show and to meet some great guys, but she understood now *why* she'd been chosen. Apparently she was going to have to compete for the attentions of the men on the show…she was going to have to compete with a woman that looked like a walking, talking Barbie doll. Marissa was beautiful. She was polished, skinny, and had a set of boobs that even Becky had a hard time looking away from.

Becky knew she didn't have a chance of getting any of the men on the show to look at her. She also knew the whole experience was going to be a let-down, but now she didn't have a choice. She'd signed the contract, she was here and she had to go on with it. She sat in a chair in her room, hands folded in her lap, and watched as a tear landed on the back of her hand. She'd never felt so alone in her life.

## Chapter Two

Becky watched as the men were introduced at the first cocktail hour. She'd felt sorry for herself for about ten minutes, then got herself under control. She was here, she might as well make the best of the situation. Maybe, just maybe some of the guys would look deeper than the surface and see *her*.

She'd been instructed to dress as though she was going on a first date, so she'd chosen a pair of khaki pants and a nice pink blouse. When she walked into the room and saw Marissa, she wanted to sink through the floor. She'd screwed up. Marissa was wearing a slinky black dress that left most of her back bare, and four inch heels. Her hair was in an up-do with small tendrils hanging down, framing her face. Becky knew she was out of her element. She looked positively frumpy standing next to Marissa. She'd been pleased with what she'd seen when she looked in the mirror before coming down the stairs, but now she felt very much like the ugly stepsister.

When the men were introduced, Becky was glad to

note that they weren't half "hunks" and the other half "nerds" as she feared and once seen on a reality show, but every one of them was very handsome.

Becky walked around the room, talking to each of the men in the room. She made a point to make eye contact with each and to try to get to know them. Even if she knew she was at a disadvantage next to Marissa, she still wanted to make the effort.

There was certainly a mix of men and professions. Becky had a hard time keeping them all straight. David and Derek were the easiest to remember because they were identical twins. She had no idea who was who, but at least she could remember their names. Becky wasn't sure what they did for a living, as they didn't stick around to talk to her for very long, they only had eyes for Marissa. There was also Ryan, Alex, Jose, Patrick and James. Again, she couldn't remember what they did for jobs, but Becky knew she'd figure it out as the show went on.

After meeting so many people, she had no idea what the other men's names were. She'd always been bad at remembering names. Someone could introduce themselves to her and two minutes later she'd have no idea how they'd introduced themselves. It was embarrassing and she was trying to work on it, but there was no way she'd remember everyone's name here tonight. She sighed.

Becky kept her eye on Marissa and saw her sitting on a couch with a circle of men around her. She seemed at ease and flirtatiously talked to each one. Occasionally, she'd touch them on the knee or the arm or hand. She had the art of flirting down to a science. The longer the evening went on, the more uncomfortable Becky felt. What was the point of this? She knew which woman the men would prefer...maybe that was it! Maybe this *would* be the end of this torture! Maybe the men would get to choose who they'd vie for and she could go home with a nice consolation prize. A girl could dream, right?

Finally their host, Robert, brought Marissa and Becky into a back room and told them they'd each be choosing seven men to stay, and the other four men not chosen would be going home. It was a lot like the singles shows she'd watched with her mom in the past, but it was weird that there were two girls this time. She guessed it was an interesting twist on the premise of the bachelor/bachelorette concept. Darn it, Becky was really hoping Robert would've told them the guys were choosing which woman they wanted to compete for and the other woman had to go home right then.

Robert asked each of them if they knew who they'd ask to stay and Marissa asked him slyly, "What if I want more than seven to stay? Can I ask Becky to use one of her slots to add one of the men I want?" After a pause she added, "And vice versa, of course." Marissa giggled, thinking her words were the funniest thing ever.

"Of course," Robert told her, "Any way you want to split up the decision you can. It's up to the two of you."

Marissa turned to Becky and said, "I think Derek and David are soooo hot. They both have to stay. I love Trevon's name. Jose is rich as hell, so he has to stay as well. I also want to keep Samuel, Ryan, Joel, Dexter, and Conner, John, and Alex because they paid the most attention to me. I don't want Ned and Carter to stay. You can choose the other three that you want to stay and two that you want to go." She shrugged as if she didn't just take over the show entirely.

At this point Becky didn't really care as she didn't know any of the men, but she also didn't want Marissa to think she could walk all over her for the entire show.

"So who does that leave?" Becky asked Marissa sarcastically.

"Duh," Marissa said with disdain. "Patrick, James, Chris, Oliver, and Tommy."

Becky didn't like Marissa all that much, but she couldn't help but be impressed with her memory of all the men's names.

Becky didn't want to make someone go home solely based on what they looked like, as that wasn't the type of person she was, but Marissa seemed to know who she wanted, and since none of the men really stood out in her eyes, she'd agree, but with conditions.

"You know you just chose eleven guys to stay when really you only get to choose seven, right?" She waited for Marissa to nod and then continued. "But since I don't know any of them that well, I'll let you have more than your fair share this time. But if in the future I want to negotiate, you'll let me."

Happy that she'd gotten her way Marissa beamed at Becky and agreed immediately. They walked back out into the main room to let the men know who would stay and who would go.

Robert lined all the men up in the typical way these things were done on reality shows, into two lines with nine men in each line. They had a platform set up so the men in back were standing taller than the men in front. Becky and Marissa stood across from the men with Robert between them.

"Welcome to *Arizona Reality!*" Robert boomed, arms spread wide. Becky inwardly cringed. Who the hell came up with the names of these shows? It sounded like they were selling a house or something.

Robert continued dramatically, "Hopefully you had a good time tonight getting to know each other. Becky, Marissa, you will each get the chance to have seven men stay to compete for your affections. Unfortunately, four of you men will be leaving tonight. Marissa, we'll start with you. Who do you want to stay tonight and get to know you better?"

Marissa, in her glory, beamed and dramatically stepped forward to give her speech. "I had such a good time tonight," she gushed, "I'm so happy to meet all of you. This is *such* a hard decision! If it was up to me I'd have *all* of you stay so I could get to know you better, but unfortunately that's impossible." Marissa pouted prettily. She named seven of the men she wanted to stay, pausing dramatically between each name.

When it was Becky's turn she felt her stomach turn. There were eleven men looking intensely at her. She really didn't want to have to disappoint any of them. She tried hard to remember who the men were that Becky wanted to keep and didn't mention. It was easier to remember the names of the men who weren't staying.

"Uh, Like Marissa said, this choice was really hard. I enjoyed meeting all of you and I wasn't sure how to decide who I wanted to stay and who I wanted to go as I don't really *know* any of you." Seeing the impatient looks on the remaining men's faces she decided to hurry and get this over with. This part of the show definitely sucked. She didn't like it when people were mad at her, and she was definitely going to make four of these men unhappy. Becky turned toward the men and rushed through the seven names, hoping she had them right, but knowing even if she didn't, it wouldn't make much difference to her. Marissa might care, but she didn't. "John, Conner, Dexter, Joel, James, Patrick and Samuel."

Becky and Marissa both jumped as Robert boomed as soon as Becky finished saying Samuel's name. "The choice has been made!"

"What the hell?" Becky heard Carter say unbelievably. "This show sucks." He snarled the words and stepped off the platform toward the front door of the huge house. He wrenched the door open and actually slammed it behind him like he was three years old.

Robert continued, even though Carter had stormed out of the house and ruined his planned dramatic delivery of his speech. "I'm so sorry Ned, Tommy, Carter, and Oliver, but you've not been invited to stay by our lovely ladies. It's time to say goodbye."

The three men who were still there came over and kissed Marissa on the cheek, shook Becky's hand and walked out. Becky felt awkward as hell as the men displayed the favoritism so blatantly. This left the other fourteen men standing in their two lines, all with goofy smiles on their faces. Becky sighed. This was going to be a *long* eight weeks.

# Chapter Three

JONATHAN WATCHED IN disbelief at the spectacle in front of him. He'd been working for about three weeks on the reality show and was beyond disgusted. It wasn't the basic premise of the show, single guys trying to get the attention of a single lady, but more the way Eddie and the other producers were making one of the women look.

Jonathan knew when the producers chose the single women the men would be competing for, they picked two women who were complete opposites on purpose. Of course, it would make for good television, but it certainly didn't mean the women were treated the same way. It wasn't as if Becky wasn't attractive, because she was, but when put side by side with Marissa, Jonathan knew most people would think Marissa was the pretty one, and Becky was the "lesser" one.

It wasn't just their looks either. It was obvious Becky was uncomfortable in most of the settings they'd put her in thus far. One week the group went to a local disco club. The music was loud, and it was hard to hear anything, even with the microphones the contestants were wearing. Jonathan's job was to follow Becky around and all he heard all night was her answering questions about Marissa and who she thought Marissa liked best. He'd been watching Becky over the last few weeks and had seen her grow less and less animated.

When he'd first seen her at the introductory meeting of the show and to let the contestants meet the camera operators, she'd seemed at ease with herself and she smiled a lot. She was certainly excited to be on the show and for it to start. She was very friendly with all of the camera operators and joked around with them. At that point she hadn't realized they weren't allowed to really talk to her much, and she'd spoken freely about how glad she was to meet them all and how happy she was to be there.

Now her smile was forced and Jonathan knew she gritted her teeth a lot. She had bags under her eyes and it was obvious she wasn't sleeping well. She no longer tried to engage with the camera operators and any time she met their eyes, she'd look away in consternation.

He could sense her frustration, embarrassment, and sadness. It went against Jonathan's nature to allow any woman to be disgraced like Becky was, but there was nothing he could do but watch through his lens. He thought he'd been jaded by Hollywood before starting this job, but this was the last straw. He was so thankful he only had one more show to get through after this one before he could start working with his brother. He wanted out of show business for good.

That night after going off duty on the set, Jonathan was sitting at Dean's dining room table, talking with his brother. He'd be working for the next three nights, so all he wanted to do was sit around and talk to his brother tonight.

"I can't believe what they're doing to her," Jonathan told Dean. "Seriously, they're making a fool out of this woman and she knows it. There's nothing she can do, but try to pretend everything is okay."

Dean looked at Jonathan carefully. "Why do you care, bro'?" he asked seriously. "It's not like she's actually being harmed, if she's experiencing a little embarrassment, she probably deserves it for agreeing to be on the show in the first place."

Jonathan looked at Dean and answered as honestly as possible. "I know. Intellectually, I know she brought it on herself by signing the contract, but you taught me to watch out for people, Dean, and I'm watching and she's hurting. I can't do anything for her and it's awful. It's like she's on an island surrounded by water and dying of thirst. I don't know." He paused, then continued, "There's something about her. She almost feels like…" His voice faded off.

"Feels like what?" Dean asked, honestly perplexed. He'd never seen his brother like this. *He* was the one in their family who usually had the need to protect others, not Jonathan. "There had to have been situations like this in California that you've seen before in the industry. Women who are being taken advantage of, who are making bad choices. Why is this so different? Do you think she's your *One*?" Dean asked seriously, sitting up in his chair with an expectant look on his face. "It'd explain the feeling…"

Every man in their family had been quick to fall in love. It was as if there was only one person in the world for them, and as soon as they saw that woman, they knew it immediately. This was the case as far back as any of them could remember. Their parents were cases in point. Both Jonathan and Dean had been told over and over the story of how they met and how their dad knew instantly their mom would be his. Of course, the women usually didn't feel the same way at first and required some wooing and courting. It was a tough thing to believe and while Dean wanted to believe he'd find his *One* just like all of his ancestors did, it was a farfetched idea. But the hope that he'd really meet someone and know on the spot she was the one for him was why he'd never been married yet. He was holding out for the fairytale, even though anyone who knew him would scoff at the very idea.

"No, no, no." Jonathan was quick to reassure him. "Believe me, she's not my *One*. It's just…I connect with her somehow, but not in a 'you're mine' kind of way. There's just something about her that makes me want to bash all the other contestants and that stupid producer upside the head for the way they're treating her." Jonathan continued trying to explain to his brother.

"You should've seen her the other day. Eddie put together a pool party for the contestants. I think it was mostly so the audience could ogle everyone in their swimsuits. Everyone in the industry knows sex sells. Marissa was in her element. She wore a skimpy white bikini and strutted her stuff all afternoon. Becky wore a one piece black suit with some sarong thing and sat at a table next to the pool all afternoon. Not one of the men asked if she wanted something to drink. Oh, some came over and talked to her, but mainly to try to pump her for information about Marissa. She had to watch as man after man brought Marissa something to drink, or a snack, or offered to rub lotion on her back, or helped her from the water when she went swimming.

"Over and over it was rubbed in Becky's face that she wasn't desirable, wasn't worth their notice, wasn't as pretty as Marissa. She had to sit there and take it all afternoon. She had a fake smile on her face the entire time the party went on. As soon as Eddie proclaimed the party over she stood up and walked back into the house and never looked back. She didn't say anything to anyone, just went straight up the stairs into her room. I'm telling you, bro', she's miserable and knows what's going on around her, but she just doesn't know how to stop it and in fact *can't* stop it."

Dean listened to his brother speak with a deep passion about this woman. It was the first time he'd ever heard him be protective about a woman in his life. Oh, he respected them, but Jonathan was more a "love 'em and leave 'em" type of man. He generally didn't concern himself about finding his *One* and settling down or about what emotions a woman might be feeling. The fact he was this concerned about this woman was curious and out of character, and made Dean want to meet her.

"You've got me interested, bro'," Dean told Jonathan honestly. "Any chance I could come to the set and visit?"

Jonathan beamed. "I was hoping you'd say that!" He pulled a guest pass to the set out of his back pocket. "You'll have to sign a confidentiality agreement before you're allowed into the production house, but I've already got it arranged!" Jonathan paused for a moment and told Dean, "Tomorrow the two ladies are going on a double date. Last week Marissa got to choose where they'd go, and this week Becky got to choose. I heard she wanted to go on a hike. I think she chose it just to irritate Marissa. I've seen her subtly do it before. She purposely chooses activities she knows Marissa will hate. She isn't obvious about it, but I know she's aware of exactly what she's doing."

"Where are they going?" Dean asked, knowing there weren't too many places around that would be appropriate.

"I think she chose Devil's Canyon," Jonathan said with a smile.

Dean smiled too. He knew the hike started out pretty tame, but quickly became quite strenuous. It was only two miles to the canyon, but after the first three fourths of a mile there was a pretty intense elevation gain.

"Maybe I'll take a rain check on that set visit," he told his brother, and when he saw him frown, quickly continued, "I think I'll visit Devil's Canyon tomorrow and check things out. I've got a hankering to take a hike."

Jonathan smiled. "Perfect! Just be sure to let them get there first. You can then meet them on the trail and watch what happens. I'm not assigned to film them tomorrow. I'll be back at the house with the other men and filming them while the ladies are on their double date. Don't be surprised at anything you might see out there. Eddie is slick and knows how to throw a curve ball at everyone. Marissa is just as bad."

Dean smilcd. "Don't worry, bro', I'll be discrete.

You've got me curious to meet both Marissa and Becky now. I'll call when I get back."

The two brothers sat for a while longer, enjoying each other's company and simply shooting the shit before heading up to bed. Tomorrow would be a long day for both of them.

## Chapter Four

BECKY SIGHED. THIS so-called date was going to suck. She'd chosen the hike option, not only because she wanted to see Devil's Canyon, but because she was annoyed at Marissa and wanted to piss her off. She should've known somehow it would end up backfiring on her. She couldn't catch a break. For the thousandth time she regretted agreeing to be on the show. It was the worst reality show in the history of reality shows, and that was saying something since there were so many bad ones on nowadays. Thank God her mom hadn't lived long enough to watch it. That was Becky's only consolation right about now, even if it made her feel like crap to actually think it.

The five of them arrived at the trailhead around ten in the morning. Marissa, Becky, the cameraman, Jose, and Alex all piled out of the van in the parking area. Jose was nice enough, at least he talked to her like she was a real person, but Alex was like all the popular kids she knew back in high school…ignoring those around him who he thought were beneath him. Becky knew he thought she was beneath him.

They'd started off on the hike and everyone was happy and acting like they couldn't imagine being anywhere else, but soon Marissa started complaining. It was too hot. It was too rocky. Her backpack was itching…anything and everything had her complaining. Becky tried to ignore her and enjoy the beautiful day. It was a perfect day for hiking and she was determined to have a good time. Right when the trail started ascending, Marissa suddenly collapsed on the ground and grabbed her ankle.

"Owwwwwww, I think I twisted it…bad!"

Jose and Alex were right there, patting her shoulder and asking what they could do to help. Becky looked at the cameraman. He had his camera pointed at the trio and the drama. She rolled her eyes, knowing they wouldn't catch it on film. She didn't really know the camera operators that well. When she met them for the first time she thought she'd be able to be friends with them, but she soon found out they weren't allowed to talk to the contestants. It bummed her out at first, but now that the show was continuing she was glad she hadn't gotten to know them. It was just too embarrassing. She'd seen some of them looking at her with pity. Becky hated that. She knew she was being made out to look pathetic on national television, but there was nothing she could do about it. She didn't know the cameraman who was with them today very well. Eddie kept moving them around so she and Marissa couldn't get to know them. Even if she wanted to talk to them, she couldn't. It was against the "rules." Eddie was a stickler for the "rules."

Becky watched Marissa bitch and moan a bit more and finally couldn't help herself, she said sternly, "Come on, Marissa, it can't hurt that badly, let's keep going."

Marissa glared up at Becky. "What do you know? It's not *your* ankle that's hurt! I can't possibly go on!"

Becky sighed. "Fine, you want to sit here and wait while we continue on?" She gestured toward Jose and Alex. "We'll pick you up on the way back." Becky couldn't believe she'd actually said it, but she was sick of sitting around letting everyone else make all the decisions for her.

"I can't possibly wait here by myself!" Marissa moaned, not surprisingly, and grabbed both Alex and Jose by an arm. "You guys'll stay here with me, right? I mean, it's not like you really *wanted* to walk around in the heat, right?"

What could the men say to that…of course they agreed.

"Fine!" Becky said, pissed off. "You guys stay here. I really want to see Devil's Canyon. It sounds fascinating and I've wanted to see it since I got here. It's not that much farther. I'll just go on up the trail, and then I'll come back and meet you here. Then we can go back to the house."

She watched as Marissa's eyes lit up with satisfaction and Alex and Jose both nodded. She looked up at the camera operator, knowing he'd be torn between following her and staying with the trio.

She said in a gentler voice to him, "You stay with them. It's not good TV to just film me walking." She winked at him, not surprised when he nodded, and she set off up the trail without looking back. It was great to get some time to herself. The only time she'd been by herself was when she'd been sleeping, and she hadn't been sleeping all that great lately anyway. The air was nice and fresh and there wasn't anyone else on the trail. It was a good day to forget all about the stupid show and what an idiot she was for agreeing to be on it in the first place. She could enjoy seeing a part of the country she'd never seen before.

Almost as soon as Becky was out of sight, Marissa started manipulating Alex and Jose into leaving. She wanted to teach Becky a lesson and having her come back and not finding them there would be a great way! She moaned that her ankle was probably really hurt and she couldn't wait for Becky to come back before seeing a doctor. She finally convinced them they needed to take her to the emergency room and they could come back for Becky. After all, it wouldn't take too long to see a doctor and Becky would be gone for such a loooong time. So the foursome, including the camera operator, walked/hobbled back to the parking area and headed for the hospital. Leaving no note for Becky and no sign they'd even been there.

※

Becky reached the top of the trail and sat down harshly on the bench. Holy crap, that was a tough hike. She knew there was no way Marissa would've made it. She would've been too concerned about her makeup and not huffing and puffing in front of the guys. It was probably good she'd been hurt before attempting the steep part of the trail. Becky didn't realize how tough it was going to be, but it was beautiful.

She gazed out at the canyon. It wasn't as big as the Grand Canyon, obviously, but it was a good size. There was a small waterfall off to the left and the color of the rocks was amazing. Becky scooted her butt forward, put her head on the back of the bench and closed her eyes, letting the warmth of the sun soak into her skin. She knew she couldn't stay there too long, Marissa would get restless and she'd have to get back, but ah, the peacefulness was a blessing.

Becky sat up when she heard a noise in the brush off to her right. She turned toward the noise, expecting to see a deer or a fox or another small animal. She couldn't believe her eyes when she noticed a huge coyote. The animal was lying in the brush, not moving, but staring at her. Becky stood up slowly and climbed up on the bench. It wasn't any protection at all, but it made her feel a bit better. The coyote was beautiful. It was black with white paws and white on its chest and the tip of its tail. It just lay there on the ground, staring at her. Becky was a bit nervous as she'd always heard coyotes were aggressive animals and the fact it was just sitting there was downright eerie. She hoped it didn't have rabies or anything. Becky stared right back at the animal. She couldn't believe she was this close to it, but it made no sudden moves and didn't even seem to be threatened by her.

She whispered, "Hello, coyote," expecting it to leap up and race away. All that happened was its tail started wagging. The coyote's eyes never left her face.

"You really aren't so big and bad, are you?" she asked nervously, not expecting an answer. "You know you probably shouldn't be here. There are way too many people that come around here, you could be in danger," Becky continued on, a little unnerved by the way the coyote kept staring at her. *Was* it rabid? Animals did odd things when they were sick. "You should go home to your mate and pups." She didn't know what gender the coyote was, but she imagined it was a male.

It was large, therefore, she reasoned, it must be male. She had no basis for thinking that, but there it was anyway.

"She must be wondering where you are…go on…you go and I'll just be on my way." Still the coyote just lay there in an unnatural way…finally Becky knew she had to get going down the trail. She couldn't stand there any longer and have a one way conversation with the animal.

"Okay, here's the deal. I have to get going…so I'm going to step down…if you promise not to eat me, I promise not to tell anyone you were here…deal?" She waited, not expecting any response, but waiting as if she'd get one anyway. She was totally shocked when the coyote backed up a bit…really it was more of a shuffle as it never really stood up, but it scooted back as if to agree with her.

Becky slowly put one foot on the ground, wishing she had her camera with her. Darn Eddie and his rules. They weren't allowed to have their cell phones or cameras while filming, which she thought was ridiculous. No one was without their camera phone nowadays. No one would ever believe this encounter with the coyote and this animal was so beautiful Becky wished she could immortalize him on film. Besides, if it attacked her, she thought morbidly, she could've always taken pictures of her mangled body to show her coworkers back home.

She put her second foot on the ground and slowly backed away from the bench, never taking her eyes off of the coyote, noticing it never took its eyes off her either. Finally Becky knew she had to turn around and watch where she was going. It was a steep trail and she couldn't walk down it backward. She took a deep breath and turned her back on the coyote…waiting. When nothing happened she looked over her shoulder as she started down the trail and saw that the coyote was gone. She knew she hadn't dreamed it, but it was uncanny how quickly and quietly the animal disappeared.

✹

DEAN CALLED JONATHAN to let him know he'd arrived at the parking lot for Devil's Canyon. "Yo, bro', I'm here at the parking area but there's no one around. Are you sure they were coming here today?"

"Yes, I know that's where they were hiking today because Eddie kept talking about how the name of the canyon was great for drama on the show," Jonathan told him emphatically. "Maybe you missed them?" he said skeptically.

Before Dean had a chance to answer they both heard a commotion on the set. "Hold on," Jonathan told him unnecessarily. "I think they're back…"

Dean waited while Jonathan listened to the pandemonium nearby. He couldn't hear what was going on, but knew his brother would let him know. Jonathan quickly came back on the phone and asked urgently and in a low voice, "Are you still at the parking lot at Devil's Canyon?" Dean didn't understand the urgency in his brother's voice but unconsciously and automatically kicked into protector mode.

"Yeah, I'm sitting here, looking at the trail head. What's up?"

Jonathan told him quietly, "I'm going to put my cell on speaker, so you can hear, but don't say anything. Becky might need your help…"

Dean's whole body clenched. Hearing that a woman needed help did that to him every time. He hadn't even met Becky, but he'd heard Jonathan talk about her so much he *felt* as if he knew her anyway. Dean suddenly heard a woman's voice in the middle of a conversation with at least one other man.

"…and I hurt my ankle really badly…so Jose and Alex volunteered to take me to the hospital…"

"Are you all right?" asked a male voice with fake sincerity.

"I am now. Luckily Alex and Jose were there! I can't imagine what I would've done out there all alone with no one to help me." Dean could just imagine the look the woman was giving the two men. She sounded whiny and manipulative to him. There weren't many things a woman could do that would turn him off, but being manipulative was one of them.

"Where's Becky?" Dean heard Jonathan ask the woman, most likely Marissa, gruffly.

"Oh, she left us. She wanted to continue on the hike. She didn't *care* that I was hurt," the woman said in a nasally voice that grated on Dean's nerves even more than it had before.

Dean heard Jonathan ask a man standing near him, presumably a camera operator, "You left her out there? By herself? At Devil's Canyon?"

"Hey, she seemed perfectly willing to go…she didn't seem to mind…." His voice trailed off and Dean could hear that he finally felt guilty for leaving Becky. The sad thing was that it had taken this long for him to feel that guilt.

"We had to get Marissa to the hospital." Alex defended their actions. "She was hurt. We knew that we'd get back here and someone could go and get Becky. I'm sure she's fine. She can take care of herself." Alex's tone was nonchalant and almost disgusted, as if a woman taking care of herself was a bad thing.

Dean had heard enough. He disconnected the call. He knew what Jonathan wanted him to do, and he didn't even have to ask. Jonathan would know he was on it. If Becky was alone out on the trail he'd be sure she made it back to the production house all right. Chances were that the woman *was* fine and there was no need to worry. He knew Jonathan had a soft spot for Becky from hearing him talk about her. He figured he'd head out on the trail, find Becky and accompany her back to the production house. He'd get to meet the woman who had Jonathan so tied up in knots as well as make sure she got back to the set with no issues.

Dean got out of his truck, grabbed his backpack, and headed over to the trail head. He'd start out on the trail and hopefully he'd run into her as she made her way back down from the canyon.

## Chapter Five

✦

BECKY LAY ON the ground and tried to orient herself. She remembered walking down the steep trail, thinking about the strange behavior of the coyote at the top…then nothing. She was at the bottom of a small ravine, obviously having slipped down the slope. She looked up and winced. Her head hurt. She saw the slide mark her body had made as it came down the side of the hill. She looked at her hands. They were pretty scraped up too. She didn't remember the fall, but obviously she'd tried to slow herself down as she tumbled.

She reached up to feel the back of her head where it hurt the most and her hand came away with blood on it. Crap and double crap. She figured she'd probably hit her head on a rock or something as she tumbled down the steep hill.

She forced herself to a sitting position and took stock. It didn't feel like anything was broken, thank God. She could move her legs and her arms with no blinding pain. She was able to move her head back and forth, although it felt like someone was pounding on her skull from the inside. She slowly turned over and got on her hands and knees. There was no use sitting there. It wasn't as if she could wait until Marissa and the guys would come looking for her.

She thought back to the coyote she'd seen earlier. If there was one, there'd probably be others and she didn't want the smell of her blood to attract other wild animals. She was lucky with the coyote at the top of the trail. She didn't want to push it. Becky knew some time had passed and Marissa would be furious for having to wait for her. She dreaded having to deal with her and her attitude with her head hurting as it was, but it would be kind of nice to at least be back with other people. They'd help her, no matter if they weren't attracted to her. She'd procrastinated enough, it was time to make her way back up the hill.

Slowly but surely, Becky crawled up the steep slippery slope. Many times she slid back down, negating her progress, but she held on to whatever she could and finally made it back to the trail. She was sweating profusely and was covered in dirt. Her hands were filthy and her clothes were also covered in smears of dirt. As far as she could tell, her head wasn't bleeding anymore, but it still hurt like nothing she'd ever experienced before. She'd tied her hair back in a messy bun at the back of her head before starting her hike. That would prevent her from feeling the stickiness of her hair where the blood had seeped through, and maybe at the same time put a bit of pressure on the wound, stopping any more bleeding. Becky glanced at her watch. Crap. Three hours had gone by from the time she'd left the group. Marissa was going to be beyond pissed, and Becky couldn't really blame her. She'd be ticked too.

Once she'd reached the trail at the top of the hill, Becky stood up slowly and felt the world tilt. She quickly knelt on the ground right there in the middle of the trail. She had to get it together. She had to get down the trail, and staying here wasn't an option. She crawled over to a nearby rock, wincing as her scraped and bruised hands landed on the rocks on the trail. She pulled herself up and sat upright. See? She could do this. She *had* to do this. She couldn't very well crawl all the way back down the trail.

Becky straightened her backpack that had miraculously stayed put throughout her mishap, and slowly brought herself upright once more. There! She was vertical. She took baby steps as she walked down the trail, keeping her head down, watching where her feet were landing, counting her steps to keep the pain of her head out of her mind. The last thing she needed was to fall over a root or rock in the path and hurt herself even more.

Becky finally got to the place where Marissa and the others had said they'd wait for her. Becky sat on the rock with a sigh. There was no sign of them. It was eerily quiet in fact. Other than the birds chipping merrily in the trees she couldn't hear signs of anyone else. What did she expect? That spoiled Marissa would calmly just sit in the wilderness bored out of her mind waiting for her? Hell no. She should've known better.

Becky eased her backpack off and leaned it against a rock, then eased herself down onto the same rock. She closed her eyes for a moment before taking her water bottle out of a side pocket of her backpack. She took a drink and tried to figure out what to do next. She couldn't quite concentrate; figuring she probably had a concussion.

Where would Marissa go? She knew she'd been gone a long time, but would they really leave her out here? No way…okay, maybe…yeah, probably. Becky sighed. She had to get to the start of the trail to the parking area. It was a long shot, but maybe they'd be there waiting for her to get back. The cameraman wouldn't leave her. There was no way. But if for some reason they weren't there maybe she could find someone to give her a ride. If no one was there *somebody* back at the show had to realize she was gone and come and get her. She was on a reality show, for God's sake. She was one of the damn *stars* of the reality show, they'd come back to get her. She just had to make it to the parking lot. She put her head in her hands and sighed. She'd get up in just a minute.

Dean walked quickly up the trail toward Devil's Canyon. He wasn't sure where along the path the woman might be, but he'd find her. It wasn't as if she could walk back to the set. She had to be out here somewhere. He had his first aid supplies in his backpack, just in case. He'd learned a long time ago to be prepared for anything.

He rounded a corner in the path about half a mile from the start of the steep incline and saw a woman sitting on a rock with her head in her hands. Dean stopped dead in his tracks. Was that Becky? She looked hurt, and his heart almost stopped. There was nothing worse than a woman who was hurt. He could handle pissed, he could handle sad, he could even handle tears, but a woman who'd been hurt made his heart ache and made his protective instincts hard to control.

He had to calm down before he scared the woman to death. He slowly made his way toward her, trying to make enough noise so she'd hear him coming and not be startled by her presence.

Becky heard someone on the trail and forced herself to look up. She was tired and not feeling well, but knew this person might be her chance to get out of there. She hadn't seen anyone else on the trail the entire time she'd been there, so if this person had a car, then she'd ask, or beg, for a ride. It wasn't the safest thing to do, but what choice did she have really? She'd have to take the chance that this person wasn't a homicidal killer.

She looked up…and up…and up at the man coming toward her. He wasn't handsome in the classical sense, but he carried himself with a sense of purpose and strength as if he wasn't scared of anything. He was wearing a pair of jeans and a plain gray T-shirt with a backpack. He was dressed for hiking. Her gaze continued upward until she met his eyes. They were dark, probably brown, but they were looking at her with an intensity she'd not been looked at before. She couldn't tear her gaze away as he came nearer. Crap, if he was a serial killer she was in big trouble, but damn, he was easy on the eyes.

Dean looked at the woman sitting on the rock on the side of the trail. She looked tired, a little scared, and a bit pissed, all at the same time. Other than her emotional state, she looked okay, until he got closer and could see blood on her hands and the collar of her shirt. Her clothes were streaked with dirt. It was obvious she'd taken a fall at some point. The blood worried him, he hoped it was nothing serious.

When she finally looked up at him he stumbled a bit as he continued toward her. Her eyes were a pale blue, almost gray in color. She was dressed plainly in a pair of jeans and a T-shirt. Her face was pale, but had swaths of red in both cheeks, probably from exertion as well as some sunburn. Since she was sitting down he couldn't see how tall she was, but she looked tiny to him. Hell, most people looked tiny to him.

But the one thing Dean thought most of all, was that she was beautiful. Sitting on the rock, looking up at him, trying not to look like she needed help. Damn. It hit him. Holy crap. She was his. His *One*.

He took a deep breath. Holy shit. It was true. All it took was one look and he wanted her more than he'd ever wanted anything. He hadn't completely believed the stories he'd heard his entire life, but it was true. A part of him still thought it was ridiculous. He didn't know anything about her. She could be a raving bitch. She could be married. She could be so many things, including *not* Becky, but it didn't seem to matter to his heart. She was his. *His*.

Dean stopped in front of the woman and watched as she tilted her head back and winced as she looked up at him. He squatted down in the middle of the trail to talk to her, not getting too close to her so she'd feel more comfortable.

"Hi," he said quietly. "Are you okay?" He wanted nothing more than to reach for her, fold her in his arms and keep her safe. She'd probably deck him if he tried it, though. He was a stranger to her after all. He might know she was his, but she had no idea. Throughout his family's history the men always had a hard time convincing their *One* that she *was* their *One*. It seemed it would be the same in his case as well.

Becky tried to smile at the gorgeous man in front of her. She furiously blushed, knowing she looked like crap. Why couldn't she meet someone like him when she was all dressed up and looking her best? Figured. "Hi, of course, just resting for a bit. It's a long hike." She mentally smacked herself in the head. She was such a dork. Just resting for a bit? Jesus, she sounded stupid even to her own ears.

She wasn't quite sure how to go about asking for help, as she didn't have to do it very often but she didn't have a choice.

"Have you seen a woman and two—no…three men back that way?" she asked, gesturing toward the direction the parking lot was in.

Dean shook his head. "No, I haven't seen anyone and my truck is the only vehicle in the lot."

Becky sighed. She figured they would've left, but it still hurt to hear her suspicions were correct. She really was nobody important on the stupid show. She tried not to let it depress her any more than she already was. After all, she knew it by the way everyone acted around her, but she couldn't help it when her shoulders sagged. Shit. Could this day get any worse?

"Can I help?" Dean asked quietly. Every bone in his body was screaming at him to pick her up, hold her close and never let her go. To tell her nothing would ever hurt her again, that he wouldn't allow it. But he knew he couldn't do it. He was a stranger. She didn't recognize him as her *One*. He had to be careful not to alienate her. He just wanted to help her.

"Can you call someone for me? I don't have a cell phone on me," Becky asked quietly, and when Dean took out his cell phone, she shook her head. "Crap…uh…never mind…sorry…I don't know the number at my friend's house," she said awkwardly. She must sound like the biggest flake.

Dean simply put the phone back in his pocket, relieved he had a reason to prolong his contact with her, and held out his hand.

"My name is Dean," he said simply. "Dean Baker."

Becky looked at the hand the man reached toward her. It was calloused and big and she wanted to grab a hold of it and never let go. She could even imagine him laying it on her cheek and brushing his thumb over her cheek. Jesus. She shook her head and figured she was feeling needy because of the last couple of weeks of not having anyone look at her like she was someone.

She reached toward his hand. "Becky Reynolds," she told him. She followed his eyes to her hand she was holding out and at the last minute took it back and hugged it to her chest. It was scraped and bleeding…there was no way she could shake his hand without it hurting. She met his eyes and shrugged apologetically.

Dean saw her hand and held his breath. It was killing him that she was hurt. It was physically hurting him as much as she probably hurt herself. He was in a pickle. This was his *One* and she was on a reality show to find a husband. How the hell was he going to get around *that*?

Dean moved slowly toward the rock that Becky was sitting on and gestured toward it as if asking permission to sit next to her. Becky scooted over and gave him some room.

Dean asked again, "Are you okay? What happened? You look a little worse for the wear," he said with a smile, hoping she'd trust him just a little. He *needed* her to trust him. He held his hand out toward her again, palm up. "Can I see your hand? I promise to be gentle."

Becky grimaced at herself. Not answering his question about letting him see her hand, she kept it close to her chest and said, "Yeah, I slipped on the trail on my way down…but I'm okay. Thanks for asking."

Dean slipped his backpack off and told her calmly, trying to sound nonchalant, "I have some basic first aid things in my bag, let me help." He kept his voice low and calm, trying once again to help her.

"I really just need to get a ride back to my friend's

house," Becky said again, trying desperately not to break down. Why was he being so nice? "I'm not hurt that badly, I can get cleaned up there," she said with a quaver in her voice.

Dean continued to hold his hand out toward her. He didn't understand why she was downplaying her injuries. By the way she was squinting he knew she had to have a headache, and there was the blood he could see on her palms and on the collar of her shirt.

"Please," he told her quietly. "Let me help you. I can at least help you wash your hands so they don't get infected. Then can you please let me take a look at your head where you hit it? I'm worried about you."

Becky cocked her head and looked at him, ignoring his comment about worrying about her, even though it sent tingles throughout her body. She asked after a moment, "How do you know I hit my head?"

Dean took a deep breath. This was killing him. Why wouldn't she just give in and let him help her? He usually admired women who were tough in the face of adversity, but he'd give anything for Becky to want to lean on him and let him take care of her. He answered honestly, "You're squinting like your head hurts, and I can see a bit of blood on the collar of your shirt. You also have some dried blood under your fingertips. I figured it had to have come from your head somewhere. If you aren't going to let me do it, please take this wet wipe and clean your hands so they don't get infected. I really want to at least check out your head to make sure it's not worse than you think it is. I'm sure you know head wounds can be dangerous."

"It's not bleeding anymore," Becky told him quietly. "It'll hold until I get back to the house."

"What can it hurt for me to take a look to be sure?" Dean insisted, about ready to be done with the back and forth between them and just take her hands into his own and take care of her whether she wanted him to or not.

Becky sighed. She really did just want to get back the house and not have to deal with this anymore. But it didn't look like this man was going anywhere anytime soon and he genuinely sounded like he wanted to help her.

"You aren't an escaped murderer, are you?" she asked him, only half kidding.

Dean shook his head and tried to look as non-threatening as he could. "Would a crazed escaped killer take the time to try to wash your hands before he killed you?" he asked with a chuckle.

Becky giggled and shook her head, wincing when the movement made her head ache again. She reached up to take the scrunchie out of her hair when Dean stopped her.

"Let me," he said as he reached for her hair.

Becky flinched as he reached toward her and she

made a conscious effort not to back away from him.

Dean noticed the flinch and paused in mid reach and asked, "May I? I promise I'll be gentle and will do what I can not to hurt you further."

At Becky's reluctant nod he reached over slowly and unwound the hairband and loosened her hair, careful not to pull on it or otherwise cause her any unnecessary pain.

Becky closed her eyes. Man, it felt good to have his hands in her hair. Even though the pain of her injury persisted; she could enjoy his hands on her. She'd never really been touched that much after her mom died, maybe hugs by some friends every now and then, and his hands were so gentle. It was pathetic that this was turning her on. She really needed to get out more. Dean removed her hair from its bindings.

She took a deep breath and smelled…him. Holy crap, he smelled good. She didn't think he was wearing cologne, because he didn't seem like the kind of man who would drown himself in a manufactured scent, but whatever soap he used must be slightly scented. He smelled like the ocean and…man. She didn't know how to describe it, but it was delicious.

Dean was trying to control himself. He couldn't believe she was here. That he'd finally found his *One*. The fact it was because she was injured was making it not quite what he'd envisioned, but it didn't matter. He'd take care of her, then figure out what came next. He'd not lose her now.

Her hair was smooth and when he ran his fingers through it, loosening it up and making sure it was all out of the scrunchie, it slid through his fingers easily.

Dean immediately felt the wound on the back of her head. It seemed pretty big and he could tell that it had bled somewhat profusely. It was still oozing just a little bit of blood, but for the most part it'd stopped and didn't look life threatening.

He took a washcloth from his pack and wet it with his water bottle. He looked at Becky. She had her eyes closed and her hands in her lap. She didn't flinch when he started cleaning her wound, but he saw her hands clench into tight fists. He knew he was hurting her, but he also knew he didn't have a choice.

"You really hit your head hard, Becky," he told her. "Are you sure you're feeling okay?"

Becky gave him a small nod.

"Will you let me take you to the hospital?" He tried again and as soon as he said the word 'hospital,' Becky jerked away from him and stood up with a wobble.

"No, I told you, I'm fine! I don't need to go to the hospital!"

"Okay, okay," Dean said soothingly. "I'm sorry. I'm just worried about that bump."

Becky sighed. Crap. She was screwing this up royally. "Really, I'm fine. I'm sorry I snapped at you. I just want to get back to my friend's house. I've had a concussion before, this isn't one. Yes, it hurts, and yes I have a headache, but nothing is rattling around in there, I promise."

She tried to smile at him. Dean couldn't smile back. He was reaching the end of his limit of letting her stand alone and not allow him to help her. He reached back into his pack and came up with a small bottle.

"How about a couple of aspirin then?" he said with a small smile. "Will you at least take these?" Becky gratefully held out her hand and took the peace offering. If he was a killer and was offering her cyanide pills or something, so be it. She'd take the chance. She *needed* those aspirin.

"Thank you, Dean. Seriously. I'm sorry I'm being such a bitch. This hasn't been the best day for me. Will you help me wash the rest of the blood out of my hair before we go? I'd rather not go back to the house with the blood in my hair." She had no idea why she was trusting this stranger, this man, like she was. It was unlike her. It was especially unlike her to want to lay her head on his broad chest and have him hold her.

"Of course, Becky, I'll do anything you want me to," Dean answered honestly. "And you're not being a bitch. As you said, you're having a bad day. Give me your hands, let's start there."

She sat back down beside him and held her hands out to him with her palms facing up.

Dean took her right hand in his and used the wet wipe to clean her palm. Because of the fall, and the subsequent climb up the hill, they were filthy. After wiping the dirt away he could see the scrapes underneath. When he was finished with that hand, he brought it up to his mouth and kissed her palm. He held his lips to her skin for as long as he thought he could get away with before placing it back in her lap and taking her left hand into his and beginning to clean it as well.

Becky curled her right hand into a fist as if she could hold the feel of his lips on her skin a little longer by the action. She'd never, in her entire life, felt the way she had when Dean had kissed her. She felt…special. Wanted. Desired. So much feeling by one simple touch of his lips. It took her breath away.

Dean finished wiping her left hand clean and kissed it the same way he did the right. He placed that hand back into her lap, took her by the shoulders and turned her away from him.

Everything he did was no nonsense and done with a purpose. Becky thought it was sexy as hell.

"Turn this way so I can get to your head easier," he told her softly as he spun her around. "Tip your head back and look at the sky. I don't want to get your shirt wet. I'm going to pour some of my water on your hair to rinse the blood out."

Becky did as he asked and closed her eyes as she looked upward. He carefully cleaned the back of her head and got as much blood out of her hair as he could. She opened her eyes when he started drying her hair with something. Oh man, if he'd taken his shirt off she didn't know what she'd do. She looked and sighed with relief, at least she tried to convince herself it was relief. He'd taken an extra shirt from his backpack and used that to dry her hair as best he could. He'd been so gentle with her. He'd done just as he said he would, and hadn't hurt her.

Dean's hands on her shoulders were gentle. Becky opened her eyes and found herself looking into his eyes. He'd knelt on the ground in front of her and was staring at her intently.

Dean looked at this amazing woman, who, thank God was his, and said seriously, "I'm worried about you. I'm not sure I can just drop you off and forget about it. Will you let me contact you? Will you let me know you're okay after today?"

Becky swallowed. Why couldn't *this* man be on the show? Then again, she figured as soon as he saw Marissa he'd probably forget all about her.

"Dean," she said hesitantly. "I'm not sure I'll be able to."

Dean cut her off. "Please, I *need* to know you're all

right, Becky," he said urgently.

Becky looked at the man in front of her. He sounded sincere and she wasn't sure what to tell him. She really, *really* didn't want to lie to him, and she was conscious of the confidentiality contract that she'd signed. But she also liked him. Here she was, covered in blood and dirt. It was irrational as hell, not to mention that she wasn't at her best at the moment, but something about him drew her in.

"I don't have a phone, and um…I'm not allowed to receive any phone calls…I'm kinda on vacation right now…but it's also kind of a job…" Her voice trailed off, realizing how dumb and flighty she sounded. She didn't want Dean to think that she didn't *want* to talk to him. "Oh, shit…here's the deal…I'm on a reality show being filmed here in Arizona," she blurted out suddenly. The hell with it, she wasn't going to find anyone to spend her life with among the choices on the show, so why not? She didn't know what she expected Dean to say but it wasn't what came out of his mouth.

"Really? Are you serious? Cool! My brother is a camera operator on that show!" Dean tried to sound as convincing as possible. It wasn't that he wanted to lie to her, he just figured it would be better if she thought he didn't know who she was.

Becky just looked at him in disbelief. A camera operator? What were the odds? "He is?" was all she could get out.

"Yes, ma'am, and that means I'll be able to have a guest pass to come to the set! That is…" He paused and suddenly looked nervous, "if you *want* me to come and see you."

Becky looked down. "Um, Dean, I don't think I'll be able to talk to you when I go back. It's, um…a dating show…and I'm only supposed to talk to the other people on the show…" She didn't want to discourage him, but she had no idea how this could work. There was no way Eddie was going to allow her to have 'visitors,' especially if it was a man.

Dean smiled at her. "You know what? Where there's a will there's a way. Now that I know where you'll be, we'll figure it out. Just know that I *want* to figure it out. Come on, let's get you back to the house so you can shower and rest. You'll feel better once you can take a nice long shower and get into clean clothes."

He carefully took her hand and helped her stand up. He kept his hand on her waist until he was sure she was steady on her feet. Then he helped her shrug on her backpack and started back down the trail toward the parking lot. He reached out and gently took her hand in his as they walked, smiling at her when she didn't protest or pull it out of his grasp.

Becky smiled back at him as she walked. Even though her head hurt and she didn't know what would be waiting for her back at the house, she felt content holding Dean's hand and just being with him. It was the oddest feeling, and she wouldn't have believed it if she hadn't been experiencing it for herself. It freaked her out on one hand, but on the other she was so tired of being treated like crap and feeling like she was nothing. She'd gladly soak up every ounce of attention she could get from this man. And it wasn't as if Dean was hard on the eyes. He was gorgeous and she got goosebumps remembering the feel of his lips on her palm.

Suddenly, she thought of something else. She was on a dating show and his brother probably knew everything that was going on since he was a camera operator. She was instantly mortified. What had his brother told him about the show already…about her? Maybe he'd known she was going to be here today and wanted to see the reality show reject. She stopped walking suddenly and pulled her hand out of his.

"Did you know I was going to be here today?" she asked Dean abruptly.

Dean looked down at Becky calmly. She was definitely riled up. "No, sweetheart, I didn't," he easily bent the truth a bit, the endearment coming out of his mouth without any thought, "I had no idea I'd meet such a beautiful woman today, or that I'd get to play a knight in shining armor," he told her honestly. "Am I happy that I met you? Definitely. Am I happy that we can't be together right now? No way, but I can wait. I know you have obligations, and believe it or not, so do I. But I feel better knowing my brother will be around in case you need him and just to keep watch over you."

Becky's forehead furrowed and she awkwardly stood in the middle of the trail. "I don't understand this. You. I don't understand you. Why would you care? I mean, you just met me, you don't know me. Unless your brother has told you about me?" she asked in a small voice, dreading his answer.

Dean wanted to beat the crap out of all the men on the show. He could tell from her demeanor and the way she asked the question she was embarrassed.

"Jonathan didn't tell me quite how pretty you are or how tough you are," he answered honestly. He didn't want to lie and tell her he didn't know anything about her, she wouldn't believe it anyway, but he certainly was telling the truth about how beautiful she was.

"Tell me, though," Dean asked, trying to slightly change the subject. "How did you end up out here alone if you're on a reality show?" He wanted to hear what she'd say.

Becky sighed and started walking again. How much should she tell him? She thought about how nice it felt to be taken care of and how wonderful his hand felt holding her tenderly as they walked along the trail. She decided to be honest with him. If he really did want to see her again she wanted to start this, whatever *this* was, off on the right foot.

"It's stupid really. I was on a double date with the other woman on the show…"

"Whoa, other woman?" Dean interrupted. "What kind of dating show *is* this?"

Becky laughed and said under her breath, "A terrible one."

She sighed again and told Dean the premise of the show, that there were two bachelorettes the men were competing for.

"So how will it end?" Dean asked seriously. "Will you both end up with a man or what?"

Becky was embarrassed she hadn't even thought about that. Was that what Eddie had in mind for the show? That they'd each end up with a perfect match? She knew *that* wasn't going to happen. The men didn't want her, they wanted Marissa. But how else could it end? Crap, she should've asked more questions of Eddie when they met and he explained how the show would go. Would it get down to one guy and *he* would pick which woman he wanted? That would just cap off her humiliation. There were just too many awful scenarios to imagine. She mentally shrugged, it was too late now.

"I have no idea," she told Dean honestly, "but you wanted to know what happened today right?" She wanted to change the subject back to his original question.

Dean nodded and Becky told him about how she and Marissa were on a double date and it was her turn to choose what they'd do on the date. She didn't feel like going into the past dates and how disastrous they were for her, it was too embarrassing. She explained how Marissa had hurt herself and how she herself had been selfish and wanted to continue on to see Devil's Canyon.

Dean told her as they walked, "It doesn't seem to me that you were the selfish one, Becky."

Becky sighed. "Well, if I'd just gone back like she wanted to when she twisted her ankle, I wouldn't have gotten hurt and stranded here today."

"Yeah, but you wouldn't have met me either," Dean said with a cocky grin, reaching out to hold her hand again.

Becky smiled hugely, at both his words and his actions. "True, very true."

After a small silence, Becky decided she'd tell Dean about her meeting with the coyote at the top of the trail. She didn't know why she wanted to share it with him, other than the fact she needed something to talk about until they reached the parking lot, and besides, she thought he might appreciate it as much as she did.

"Something did happen to me on the trail, though," she started, looking up at Dean while they walked.

"Are you okay?" he immediately asked, concerned.

She laughed and squeezed his hand lightly. "Nothing like that, I saw the most beautiful coyote while I was up there."

Dean stopped and looked at Becky with surprise. "You did?"

"Yes, it was at the top of the trail. It's beautiful there and everything was quiet and I heard something and looked over and there he was. Just sitting in the grass."

"Were you scared?" Dean asked her quietly. Most women would have freaked out and screamed or something. Not his Becky. He smiled, he liked that. *His* Becky.

"Not really. Well, I was at first, but he just lay there, looking at me. He didn't make any moves toward me. It was really peaceful, actually."

Dean continued to smile at her. She was amazing. She was sensitive, and beautiful and tough, as he'd told her earlier.

"That sounds like it was a very fortunate meeting, Becky. You do have to be careful though, as you can't trust all wild animals." He felt compelled to say something about her trusting that coyote, even if it didn't do anything threatening.

"I know," Becky told him. "I'm not an idiot, but he wasn't scary in any way. It was as if he fit into the atmosphere and I didn't get any wild vibes from him! I was afraid for a moment it was rabid, but it wasn't drooling or doing anything other than just lying in the grass, watching me. He was beautiful. I feel fortunate for being able to have had the experience. It's hard for me to even think about how some people never will get to experience anything like this because they live in cities."

"I knew I liked you for a reason," Dean said mysteriously as they continued walking.

Becky heard the teasing note in his voice and laughed, not knowing exactly why. "And why is that, good sir?" She teased right back.

"My parents live near here and operate a wild animal refuge. They have a huge area just for coyotes that have been hurt or need relocating because they won't stop harassing the local ranchers. They aren't pets, but they're given a place to roam and run and be free, but still be protected at the same time."

Becky just looked at Dean in amazement. "Are you kidding?" she asked quietly, coming to a stop.

Dean stopped too, since they were holding hands and he didn't want to let her go. "No. I'm not kidding," he told her, wondering why she seemed so shocked.

"All my life, from the time I was a little girl," Becky started, looking into his eyes as she spoke, "I've wanted to help animals. I had this grand idea that I'd buy a piece of property and start taking in dogs and horses and pigs and cats and llamas and hamsters and whatever other animals were in need of help. My mom was constantly trying to take care of mice and birds and any other small animal I brought home that needed saving. I saw so many homeless and abused animals growing up, it broke my heart. I've never been able to get anywhere near accomplishing that goal. But to hear that your family…" Her voice broke and she couldn't go on.

Dean didn't hesitate but gathered Becky in his arms to comfort her. Finally. She was in his arms. She was the perfect height. Her head fit right under his chin and she felt so good against his chest, against his heart.

"My family does what they can," he told her, murmuring into her hair at the top of her head. "They take in all the animals they can and have a whole staff to help them. I'd love for you to meet them and to meet all the animals someday." He realized suddenly there was nothing more he wanted to do than bundle her up and take her home to meet his folks. They'd love her.

"Really?" Becky said skeptically, leaning back to look up at the man holding her in his arms. God, it felt good there. She was feeling emotionally shaky and his arms holding her close were just what she needed. For whatever reason it didn't even feel weird. With other men she'd dated it had taken quite a few dates before she'd let them get this close. Why Dean was different she had no idea, but she really liked being in his arms.

"Really," Dean said. "When you're done with your

show I'll take you to meet them."

Becky didn't know what to say. It'd be a dream come true for her to be able to visit the animal sanctuary, but she didn't understand why Dean would even offer it. It wasn't as if they actually knew each other. It'd been what, only about an hour since they'd met? But deep down Becky knew why he'd made the offer. There was some connection between them. She could feel it and she assumed he could too. What truly sucked was that she couldn't do anything about it right now. She had obligations…but God she wished Dean was on the show. Although, if he was, with her luck, Marissa would kick him off just for showing any attention to her.

They started walking again and it wasn't too much longer before they'd made it back to the parking lot. Dean helped Becky into his truck and walked around to the driver's side. Before he started the engine he looked at Becky.

"Seriously, Becky," he said, getting back to something he'd said earlier and she'd blown off. "If you need a friend or anything else, please let my brother know and he'll get in touch with me and I'll get it for you. I'll point him out when we get back so you'll know who he is. It'll make me feel better. I've never been on a reality show, but I can imagine it can be a lonely experience."

Becky looked down at her hands. Man, he was intense, but she liked it. It seemed as if he honestly wanted to take care of her. "Thank you, Dean," she told him with emotion in her voice. "Trust me, you don't ever want to be on a reality show. It *does* get lonely, but I'm not sure I'll need anything. I appreciate the sentiment though."

She wasn't sure what was in store for her on the show, but she also wasn't sure she'd actually be able to contact anyone about anything when she was back on the set. Unfortunately, Becky also wasn't sure about the connection she seemed to have with Dean. She figured once he talked to his brother, *really* talked to him about the show and about her, and once he saw Marissa, his attention would most likely wane.

Soon enough they were pulling up near the house and the set. There was a lot of activity, as usual, but nothing out of the ordinary. Becky guessed that perhaps no one had missed her yet…or cared she was gone. She sighed, trying not to get sucked back into the doldrums just seeing the house tried to push her into.

"Go ahead and stop here," she told Dean as they got close to the gate.

"I'll bring you all the way to the door," Dean told her, not liking the thought of dropping her off and letting her go back to the set on her own. Not because he thought she couldn't do it on her own, but because he wanted to lend her moral support for what waited her inside.

"Please don't," Becky said. "Seriously, I'm not supposed to talk to anyone off the set, especially someone like you." Her voice trailed off.

"Someone like me?" Dean asked, seriously wondering what she'd meant.

Becky blushed. "Yeah, someone as good looking as you." She smiled in his direction.

Dean laughed. "I'm just a regular guy doing a good deed," he told her.

Becky got serious again. "No, really, you aren't just a regular guy. Most regular guys I know wouldn't have done what you did for me today, or at least they wouldn't have been as gentle and patient. Besides, I don't want you to get in trouble, and it'll just be easier if you let me out here and let me go up by myself. I'll tell them I took a taxi home and they'll believe it."

"Most regular guys *would* have done what I did for you today, sweetheart," Dean said earnestly. "You've just been hanging around the wrong kind of men."

"Obviously," Becky agreed softly, not looking away from him. When Dean looked inclined to continue trying to persuade her to let him bring her up to the house, she simply looked him in the eyes and said, "You need to stay here. Please." She tried to sound firm, when she really felt anything but. "You can tell me what your brother looks like so I'll know it's him." *So I can try to avoid him.* Becky thought to herself.

Dean sighed, pulled over to the curb and shut off the engine. He told her to stay put, got out and walked around the truck to her door and opened it. He didn't step away when she turned sideways to slide out of the seat, but instead put both arms above his head on the door jam and leaned against the truck toward his woman. He would've rather put his hands on her body, but knew it was too soon for that intimate of a gesture. He tried to put into words what he felt, how serious he was about her.

"This isn't the end for us, Becky. You might as well know this now, you might be on a reality show, but I aim to be an unofficial contestant. I've never felt about someone the way I feel about you, even though we've only just met. I want to spend more time with you and I want to get to know you. I want you to get to know me. Just please tell me you won't forget about me while this damn show is being taped. I want a chance with you."

Becky just looked at Dean. She thought his little speech was the most romantic thing anyone had ever said to her. She cleared her throat twice before she could answer him.

"Dean, I'm not sure what to say. I…I want to get to know you too, but I'm only here for this show…I don't live here…I—"

Dean stopped her simply by putting his finger to her lips.

"Just tell me I'm not alone in this," he begged. Him, begging. He knew if his brother or friends could see him now they'd laugh their asses off. This moment meant more to him than anything ever had in his life. If she rejected him he wasn't sure what he'd do.

"You're not alone," Becky whispered shyly.

Dean leaned down and kissed her. Softly, lightly, on the lips. For a first kiss it left a lot to be desired, but he'd take what he could get and he didn't want to rush or scare her.

As soon as Dean's lips touched hers, Becky wanted to sink into the kiss and never come up for air. Unfortunately, it was a short, sweet kiss, definitely not the type of kiss Becky longed for from this man. Damn. She had it bad.

Dean ran the back of his fingers down her cheek and then slowly backed up and held out his hand for her. She gripped his hand and he helped her out of the truck.

"Be careful, sweetheart," he whispered. "Remember, if you need anything find my brother, Jonathan. He's about my height, has dark hair, long, down to the middle of his back, you can't miss him. He'll get in touch with me and we'll help you with whatever you need." At her skeptical look he put his hand at the back of her neck and pulled her toward him gently. "Seriously, Becky. Anytime. For any reason."

He watched her nod, gave the back of her neck a

quick squeeze and backed away toward the front of his truck. He watched as Becky backed toward the house…both of them reluctant to break eye contact. Finally, she turned and let herself in through the gate, then disappeared. Dean got in his truck and drove off toward his house. He'd wait for his brother to get home, and they'd make a plan.

# Chapter Six

✴

When Becky arrived back at the production house she'd explained to Eddie that she'd been hiking and when she got back to the parking lot she had to wait for someone to show up so she could call a taxi. Eddie didn't seem to care, only saying absently, "Next time don't leave the group. That's not the way this show works. You don't get to go off on your own."

*What an asshole.* Becky thought to herself while nodding at Eddie. She went up the stairs to her room to shower and get ready for dinner.

Jonathan stood off to the side and listened as Becky explained what happened to Eddie and knew there had to be more to the story, but he didn't say a word as the attention in the house quickly turned back to Marissa and her "hurt" ankle. Jonathan knew Becky was hurt as well because he could see blood on the collar of her shirt and that her hands were scraped up. He watched as she went up the stairs. There was no rule that said that the women had to stay in the common area with the men at all times, and he figured she was going to take a shower.

That night at the mixed dinner—with both the women and the men eating together—Marissa ruled the table with her story about what happened to her and the men ate it up. Jose sat next to Becky at the table and seemed to be feeling guilty about leaving her behind. Out of all the men at least he seemed to feel bad about what happened, although he *did* still leave her stranded on the trail while he tried to play rescuer to Marissa.

Watching through his camera lens, Johnathan heard Jose apologize to Becky about leaving her behind. He didn't know if Jose *really* felt bad or if he wanted to butter up Becky for the ceremony that would be held later that night. He shrugged and turned back to his camera, concentrating on getting the best shot of the contestants eating and scheming during dinner.

Marissa and Becky met in the conference room before the ceremony that night to discuss their choices for which men would be staying and which would be leaving. There were going to be two men leaving and Marissa wanted Jose to leave. She'd decided he wasn't as attentive to her as the others and she wanted him gone.

Becky wasn't surprised. Jose hadn't fawned all over her at dinner and since he'd showed *her* some attention, of course Marissa wanted him to leave. Becky almost rolled her eyes. The whole show was a farce and ridiculous. The fact that Eddie was making her and Marissa work "together" to decide who'd be leaving was creating more and more friction between them. Becky didn't think Marissa was a bad person. She was just caught up in the competitive nature of the show. Marissa could vote off whoever she wanted, Becky would do what she wanted and the hell with what Marissa wanted her to do.

Becky decided enough was enough, she was done letting Marissa make all the choices on the show. None of the men there might be attracted to her, nor she to them, but she'd be damned if she let the one man who'd actually shown some speck of thoughtfulness to her leave just because Marissa was acting like a small spoiled child. How she wished Dean could've been there. Although, she thought for what seemed like the hundredth time, that if he was, he'd probably be just as gaga over Marissa as the others.

Robert did his typically dramatic entrance for the ceremony. He asked Marissa and Becky some questions about their day and then turned to get some thoughts from the men who were left as well. Marissa once again went first and named the men she wanted to stay on the show. Then it was up to Becky to choose who she wanted to say. She voted to keep Jose and because Alex wasn't listed in her group of who was staying, he had to leave. Becky did it purposely just to piss Marissa off.

"The choice has been made." Robert boomed his

line right after Becky named her last guy, once again with great dramatic affect. Even though they knew it was coming, it still startled both Becky and Marissa. Dammit. Becky hated when he did that.

Marissa stormed up to Becky after the ceremony. "What the hell was that?!?" she shrieked. "You *knew* I liked Alex, and you *knew* I wanted Jose to go! You bitch!"

"Look, Marissa." Becky tried to say calmly and rationally. "You don't get to make all the decisions on this show. I liked Jose, and I want him to stay. It's as easy as that. We only get to pick who we want to stay, not who goes. Since you didn't pick Jose, I had just as much right to ask him to stay as you did. I'm not going to go with whatever you want. I warned you before."

"You'll pay for that, you heifer!" Marissa said ominously, obviously trying to be threatening.

Becky ignored her, turned her back and went up to her room. She didn't care anymore. She couldn't even think about the stupid men on the show, about how ridiculous Marissa was being, or about the ceremony. Her head still throbbed from her fall, and all she wanted to do was sleep.

As she lay in bed the last thing she thought about before she fell asleep was Dean and the way he'd looked at her so intently when he said he wanted to see her again. It was the type of look she'd always dreamed she'd get from a man, but never figured she would.

⭒

Jonathan knew Dean would be waiting for him when he got back to Dean's house. It was around ten at night and he wanted to hear what Dean had to say about what happened at Devil's Canyon. He knew Dean was probably the one who gave Becky a ride home, but he'd kept his mouth shut. For one thing, no one ever asked a camera operator for his or her opinion. He'd noticed another operator paying close attention to Becky and her conversation with Eddie, but he wasn't sure of her name. He knew she was attractive, but he hadn't had any time to get to know her. They'd always been put on different assignments so far on the show. He forgot all about the woman when he walked into the house and saw Dean sitting on the couch, staring off into space, not even watching the television that was on low in front of him.

He turned and looked at Jonathan when he'd walked in and simply said, "It's her."

Jonathan knew exactly what his brother meant. "Wow. What are you going to do about it?" he asked curiously.

Finding their *One* was a huge deal in their family, but Dean and Becky had more than the usual amount of obstacles in their way. She didn't live in the area and was on a reality show. Jonathan wasn't even sure where else to start with the issues they had.

"I was hoping you'd help me, bro'," Dean told Jonathan.

Without hesitating, Jonathan returned, "Of course, you don't even have to ask. At least now I know why I was drawn to her earlier. Not because she's mine, but because she's family."

Dean nodded. He knew what he meant. While Jonathan might not be sexually attracted to Becky, somehow he knew she belonged in their family.

If Becky was in trouble, once she and Dean got married, Dean knew Jonathan would lay down his life for her. It was the way it was. He'd do the same once Jonathan found his *One*.

"Tell me what really happened out there," Jonathan asked, settling down on the easy chair across from his brother.

Dean recounted the story of how he'd found Becky sitting alone on the trail and her wounds.

"She's amazing, Jonathan," Dean said, unable to hold back his praise. "I've rarely met another person, let alone a woman, with that kind of fortitude and courage. She didn't cry once, she glossed over her injuries as if they weren't hurting her. She's not one to complain. I'll have to watch her carefully in the future so she doesn't hurt herself further by ignoring something that really could be wrong."

Jonathan nodded. "I've noticed that about her while watching her on the show. It's as if the more those around her complain, the less she does. It's confounding. She'd prefer to fade into the background than bring any attention to herself."

Jonathan proceeded to tell Dean about the night on the set and the most recent ceremony. "You would've been so proud of her, Dean. She finally stood up to Marissa, and boy was Marissa pissed. It took everything I had not to laugh at the look on her face when Becky said she wanted Jose to stay."

Dean had a hard time finding any enjoyment in the fact that not only was Marissa apparently pissed at his woman, but hearing about Becky choosing another man, even in the context of defying Marissa, made him crazy. She was *his*, dammit. This was torture.

"How did she look? Did she get a shower? Was she able to see a doctor at all?"

Johnathan said that while Becky looked tired, she was holding her own and seemed to be okay. The shower she'd obviously taken when she got back to the set did her a lot of good. She never said anything about needing medical attention and Eddie apparently didn't even notice the scrapes on her hands.

"I told Becky she could get in touch with you if she needed anything and you'd tell me, but I'm not sure she will. She's independent and has a lot of honor. She knows she signed the confidentiality agreement and I'm not sure she'll break it. She's not one to ask for help, but I need to see her, to talk to her." Dean looked at his brother expectantly.

"I know, I'll see if I can't get to her tomorrow and talk to her. What if we take her one of those disposable cell phones? You know the contestants have no access to phones or computers, but if I can get her a cell, then you can call her or she can at least get in touch with you directly if she needs you, or wants to talk to you." Jonathan suggested.

"That's a great idea." Dean enthused. "I'll go out in the morning and pick up a phone for her." The two brothers sat in a companionable silence for a while.

Dean broke the silence. "I appreciate your help, Jonathan. I have a bad feeling about the show, and I have no idea why. I don't know if it's because I can't be near her, or if it's because of all that you've told me about what's happening on the set, or what. I don't want any of the men near her, especially if they're only using her to get near Marissa."

"She's tough," Jonathan told his brother seriously. "I'm sure she'll be fine. We'll work out a plan so you can talk to her throughout the show. That should make you feel better."

Dean nodded and Jonathan suddenly sat up and

said excitably, "I have another idea…what do you think?" He proceeded to outline his plan to Dean.

"I love it!" Dean exclaimed, thrilled that he'd be able to be closer to Becky over the next few weeks. They'd put the plan into action the next day. He'd get to see Becky sooner rather than later. He couldn't wait to see the look on her face when he strolled onto the set. She'd be surprised all right!

## Chapter Seven

THE NEXT MORNING Jonathan went into work earlier than normal and requested to meet with Eddie to put their plan in action.

"Hey, Eddie," he started, trying to look serious and trustworthy. "I heard about this wealthy local guy who's interested in the reality show business and wants to take a look at this show. I heard he was interested in backing your next show in the future."

It was like waving a red flag in front of a bull. Eddie's nose flared and Jonathan swore he could even see his eyes dilating.

"Who is it? Do I know him? Do you know how to get in touch with him?" Eddie was asking his questions so fast he wasn't giving Jonathan time to answer any of them. He was conceited, rightly so, since his last reality show, *Love in the Outback*, was a huge hit.

"I don't know him directly," Jonathan lied easily, "but I was able to get his name and number for you." He handed over a piece of paper with Dean's name and phone number written on it. He was sure Eddie wouldn't take the time to actually investigate Dean and would take him at his word. Jonathan had no idea how he'd made it as far in show business as he had. Oh, well. As long as it would insure Dean unlimited access to the set and the house and Becky, all was good.

Jonathan watched as Eddie quickly stepped out of the room and headed off to make the call, visions of dollar signs dancing in his head.

✹

Becky was sitting in the house's common area, reading a book when a commotion caught her eye. She looked over and saw Eddie talking to a man at the door. She looked back at her book. She wasn't interested in the comings and goings of people from the house. She was actually bored and only half interested in her book, but Marissa wasn't out of bed yet and there wasn't anything planned for the day, as far as she knew, so she tried to entertain herself. Lord knew the guys who were hanging around weren't entertaining her. They'd barely said two words to her this morning. She would've loved to have taken a walk, but that wasn't allowed. She wasn't allowed out of the house without an escort…i.e. a camera operator and an agenda.

She was so engrossed in her book and so used to ignoring the production staff around her that she was startled to hear Eddie addressing her while standing next to the couch. She looked up and almost choked. What the hell? What was Dean doing there? Was he getting her in trouble? Was *he* in trouble? Had Eddie found out about yesterday?

Dean watched as Becky tried to process his presence on the set. He wished Eddie would hurry up and get on with it so she could relax. He could feel her tension, her worry and dismay, and he wanted to reassure her that everything was okay, but he had to wait until he was introduced as he wasn't supposed to know her yet.

"This is Dean," Eddie said importantly.

Becky put her book down and stood up uncertainly, waiting for Eddie to continue speaking. God, Dean was just as hot today as he was yesterday. She nervously smoothed her hair behind one of her ears. God, did she look okay? Why hadn't she spent more time on getting dressed today? Crap, Eddie was talking, she had to pay attention rather than continue to stare at Dean and imagine what he looked like without his shirt on.

"He's an investor and is interested in funding my next show. He'll be hanging out watching the production of the show. Dean, this is Becky, she's one of the stars."

Dean held out his hand to Becky. He couldn't wait to touch her again, to feel her skin on his. Her skin looked so soft today. She looked healthy and full of life.

He thought she looked good on the trail, sweaty and hurt, but now? Wearing comfortable clothes and relaxing on the sofa? Whoa. God, he had to get it together. If he wasn't careful he'd embarrass himself, and Becky, by getting hard in front of Eddie. He shifted a little, telling himself to cool it and waited for Becky to grasp his hand.

Becky took Dean's hand and almost jolted at the feeling of his hand against hers. Again, she marveled at how it just felt right. How she felt safe with his hand wrapped around hers. Why did she feel that way? It wasn't normal, but damn it felt good.

"N-nice to meet you, Dean," she said softly, trying to sound as if she was meeting him for the first time and she hadn't had his lips on hers not too long ago.

"The pleasure's all mine," Dean told her with a smile and secretly squeezed her hand before reluctantly letting go.

Eddie continued to beam at Dean as if he was his new best friend. "Come on, I'll show you around. Marissa will be down in a bit and you can meet her too."

As Eddie pulled him away, Dean looked back and mouthed, "Later" at Becky. She sat down with a plop on the couch. She was glad to see him, but shocked at the knowledge that he was an investor…or was he? She wasn't sure she wanted him hanging around the set. She was already embarrassed at most of the things that went on, she didn't think she could stand for Dean to witness her humiliation as well as everyone else.

And then there was Marissa. Dean was good looking—okay, he was hot as hell, and even though he wasn't a part of the show, she knew Marissa would set her sights on him too. She tried not to think about it, she'd already thought about it more than was healthy, but she couldn't help herself. She thought he'd probably forget all about her once he met Marissa. Most men did. Overall she didn't think this was a good idea at all.

A bit later as Becky was going upstairs to change out of her "lounging" clothes and into her "show" clothes she was stopped by a camera operator. It was Dean's brother. She could tell by his long hair and his resemblance to Dean, and he matched the description Dean had given her the night before to a tee. She hadn't ever gotten a good look at him in the past because the camera was always in front of his face.

"Becky, my brother wanted me to give you this," and he slipped a disposable cell phone into her hand. "In case you need him, or me, our numbers have been programmed in. Be sure to keep it to yourself so Eddie, the director and the other contestants don't find out about it. It's also been set on vibrate so you don't have to worry about the noise alerting anyone to the fact that you have it."

Becky looked at the phone in her hand and then back up at Jonathan in confusion. What was going on? Why would she need a phone? She was already confused about why they thought she'd need to contact them in the first place. It was all very confusing. She slipped the phone into her pocket.

The baffled look on her face must have been telling because Jonathan said softly and urgently, "Look, my brother really likes you, and he wants to keep in touch with you, that's why he's on the set. He's definitely *not* investing in any reality shows. It's just an excuse to be here with you. He just wants to get to know you. He's also a bit protective. He wants to be sure you have a way of getting a hold of someone outside this silly show…" He paused a bit to clear his throat. "…in case you need anything. And Becky…" He hesitated again, not really knowing how to say this next part, but wanting to say something to let her know she wasn't alone. "Not every man is as shallow and dense as the men on this show are…give Dean a chance…" He didn't give her time to respond as he turned and went the other way.

Neither Jonathan nor Becky saw the camera woman quietly standing at the end of the hall. She smiled and then disappeared into a nearby room as soon as Jonathan turned and walked away.

Becky clenched the phone in her pocket tightly. Wow, Jonathan and Dean were intense, but they were straightforward and didn't seem to hold back what they were thinking. That felt so good right now because it seemed like everyone else she'd been around over the last few weeks never said what they really meant and they were all out for themselves. She wanted to feel embarrassed all over again about the show and what had been going on, but she couldn't really.

Jonathan's words meant a lot to her. It was hard to live in a "reality bubble" and not get sucked into what was happening around her all the time. It'd be great to have a link to the outside world just in case she needed it. She tried to imagine herself calling Dean just to chat and just couldn't quite make it work in her head. She knew she'd never call him out of the blue. It just wasn't in her nature to make the first move toward a guy. It did make her feel better to think Dean thought enough about her to want to give her a way to contact him or his brother. It lifted her spirits. She'd try to hold onto that feeling throughout the outing that was planned for the day. It was gonna suck. She knew it.

✸

Dean sat and watched the dynamics of the people on the show. He was expecting Marissa to be horrible after what Jonathan had told him about the show, but it was hard to truly explain to someone who hadn't met her and hadn't seen how she acted, how bad she really was.

He was sure she was a nice person, well, relatively sure, but on the show she presented a catty possessive side. She wanted all the men on the show to pay attention to her and she made sure to put Becky in a bad light whenever she could.

Dean knew Becky was embarrassed to have him there, but he wanted to be sure to let her know that she had an ally. It didn't seem like anyone else, especially not the director or Eddie or Robert, cared about her feelings. And the men on the show seemed to be just as bad. He honestly didn't understand how they could not look past Marissa's mechanisms and see that she was poison. How could they not see the beautiful person Becky was? Yes, she was his *One* and he was biased, but he'd always preferred a woman who was confident and beautiful on the inside to someone who was only beautiful on the outside.

✶

BECKY WAS BEYOND embarrassed. It was bad enough she had to endure the social events on the show, but now that Dean was there, it was worse. Holy crap. She went over in her head what she'd rather be doing at this very moment other than being on this show and having the man she wanted to like her, with every fiber of her being, watching her being humiliated. Gynecologist exam, dentist, having a broken arm set…geez, the list could go on and on.

She was sure at any time he'd walk out never to come back. Hell, she wouldn't blame him. Recently she'd been dreaming about walking out almost every day.

She'd watched Marissa meet Dean with dismay. Just as she thought she would, Marissa simpered and fawned all over him. To be fair, Dean hadn't seemed to give her any outward encouraging behavior. He was only polite, but Becky had learned the hard way that just because a man was nice to you didn't mean he meant it. She'd seen it happen over and over on the show. The men seemed to want to get to know her, but inevitably conversation would always turn to Marissa and what she thought of the other men.

This afternoon she and Marissa and their "dates" would be going to the spa. This was one of Marissa's choices of activities for the day, no big surprise there, and Becky knew she'd be miserable. There wasn't anything about a spa that she enjoyed. She didn't like having gobs of makeup put on, she knew her hair didn't hold a style very well because it was thin, and she'd never enjoyed getting a massage. On top of that her nails were short and her feet were so ticklish that pedicures were pure torture. The only good thing about the day would be that Dean wouldn't be there. Becky sighed. Since they were going off-set only the Director,

Eddie and the camera operators would be accompanying them.

As Becky and Marissa and their dates were leaving the house, Becky couldn't help but look back toward Dean and found him looking right at her. The intensity in his eyes startled her for a moment, but also warmed her from her head to her toes. He gave her a small secret smile as she walked out the door.

God, that smile could keep her going for hours. Becky smiled to herself and turned to get into the van to travel to the spa only to meet Marissa's scowling face.

"You really don't think *he* is interested in *you*, do you?" she said snidely. She didn't say anything else as the men from the show were getting into the van. She knew when to keep her cattiness to herself and when to act like Becky's best friend.

Becky knew she wasn't done with the conversation. Marissa would never let the fact she saw a man pay attention to Becky, and not herself, go without making a big deal about it. Becky knew she'd probably come up with all sorts of reasons why the look Dean sent her wasn't what it looked like. Becky didn't care. The promise and heat in Dean's eyes when he looked at her was honest and hot as hell.

Becky blocked out the inane conversation going on between the other contestants on the way to the spa and daydreamed about Dean. She imagined them on a real date, just the two of them. He'd hold her hand and kiss her throughout the date as if he couldn't help himself. At the end of the night he'd walk her to her door, back her up against it and start kissing her. His hands would roam her body and when things would start to get inappropriate he'd pull away and ask if he could come up for coffee. Just as Becky was imaging what would happen when they went inside, Eddie announced that they'd arrived. Darn.

Once they exited the van and went inside the high-end spa, Becky and Marissa were whisked away, with their camera operator in tow, toward the ladies room where they'd change into their robes and be ready to be pampered for the afternoon. Becky saw the camera operator following them into the dressing room was a woman. She wasn't very tall, but Becky could see she was extremely muscular. She figured she'd have to be in order to hold a camera on her shoulder all day.

Becky and Marissa had been signed up for the "couples" spa day, which meant they'd spend the day side by side with their dates, and each other, while being pampered. Becky wondered if the men were as reluctant for the day as she was. Probably not. Becky figured they were probably scheming to get Marissa alone at some point, preferably when she didn't have many clothes on, and wondering if they could ditch her. Derek and James didn't really seem to be the "spa" type of people, but in order to "win" Marissa she knew they'd do whatever they had to do.

As soon as they were alone in the dressing room Marissa lit into Becky, finally able to let her true self show through since there weren't any men around to see her actions.

"Seriously? You think he likes *you*?" she snarled. Repeating what she'd said earlier. "From what I've heard he's as rich as hell and there's *no* way your mousey fat ass could attract him. Just give it up. Besides, if you so much as *try* anything with him I'll report you to Eddie so fast it'll make your head spin. You're under contract, just like me, and if you screw this show up for me I'll sue your ugly ass so fast you won't know what hit you." Marissa wound down with a glare.

Becky just looked at her. Wow, that was harsh, even for Marissa. She wasn't sure what bug had gotten up her butt but she was sick of being stomped on by her and the other men on the show. It wasn't as if she and Dean had lay down on the ground and started going at it—okay, that *was* a great image, but seriously. If one look from a man toward her and not toward Marissa could make her turn into this bee-otch from hell, she had no idea what Marissa would think if any of the men actually dared to actually kiss her.

She'd had enough of Marissa's attitude. "Just because I don't have boobs out to here," Becky said, gesturing about a foot in front of her chest, "and just because I don't simper over every single thing everyone here says, doesn't mean I can't attract a man. I'd rather someone like me for who I am rather than what I look like or what I wear. And if you think for a *minute* that the men on this show like you for who you are, you're crazy. They're after the money and fame, just as you are. I guaran-damn-tee you won't have a happy-ever-after ending with anyone here. Oh, you'll both play the same game and pretend you're madly in love, but your relationship will end, just like all the others have."

Becky took a breath, interrupting Marissa when she was about to snap back at her.

"So you just keep on pretending you're little Miss Perfect and that you'd happily end up with any of those men. I'll keep playing my part and you can "win" this stupid reality show, but if you *ever* get in my face again you'll wish you hadn't. Just leave me alone, Marissa. You play the game your way, I'll play it mine and we'll go our separate ways. If you can't handle another man even *looking* at me without losing your shit, I feel sorry for you."

And with that parting shot Becky tightened the belt on her robe and slammed out of the locker room, leaving Marissa standing there with her mouth open. She hadn't expected Becky to push back.

It had felt *good*. She wasn't one to speak her mind

like that, but Marissa had pushed her too far. Some of what Marissa had said hurt, but she tried to forget about it. She was a bitch, she just had to keep reminding herself of that. What really pissed her off was Marissa belittling what she'd started to feel for Dean and to insinuate there was no way she could ever keep his attention. That hit a bit too close to what she was feeling for herself and had tried to push to the back of her mind. She knew she couldn't compare to Marissa in the looks department, but damn it, she was a good person and she certainly wasn't a troll. So what if she didn't cake on makeup or wear designer clothes, or weigh under a hundred and twenty pounds. Not everyone in the world did, and *they* still ended up happily married. She'd tolerate the day and get through it, get through the show and go back to her boring life, the way she liked it. Even if it killed her.

Becky took a deep breath and was about to head out to where Derek and James were waiting with Robert and Eddie and who knows who else from the show, when she noticed the camera woman come out of the dressing room. The camera was hanging at her side for once, and she looked Becky directly in the eyes.

"Good for you, Becky!" she said unexpectedly. "That bitch has had that coming for a long time now."

Becky could only stare at her. Finally, she managed, "Uh…thanks?"

The camera operator laughed and took a step toward Becky. She didn't hold out her hand in greeting, probably because she was worried someone would see them, but she came closer so they could talk quietly. "My name is Kina. Me and most of the other camera operators have been rooting for you from day one. Most of us were together in Australia and couldn't believe the crap that went on behind the scenes with the women on the show. Marissa would've fit in perfectly with that bunch. But thank God Alex and Sam were able to work through all that crap and find each other in spite of the way all the others acted."

Becky again could only stand there and nod. She'd watched *Love in the Outback* and didn't really understand how Alex and Sam even ended up together, since Sam was kicked off the first week.

Kina seemed to understand Becky's confusion because she continued speaking. "Becky, Sam wasn't really kicked off the first week. She made it at least half way through the show. Eddie and the other producers only edited the show to make it *seem* as if she left that early. Alex and Sam had plenty of time to get to know each other. Sam even saved my life on the set one day."

"What?" Becky exclaimed fascinated. Crap, she didn't have time to listen to the story, but God how she wanted to. It sounded like it was an amazing story. She looked behind her at where the others would be gathering and heard Kina speak again.

"I know, this is a bad time to even have brought it up, sorry. But I wanted you to know that we're all rooting for you. Don't let Marissa get you down. You have a friend in each one of us. When she's acting all bitchy look into the camera and see us standing behind the lens and know that we're cheering you on."

Becky had no idea what to say to the woman, but she didn't have to say anything. Kina hefted the camera back up to her shoulder and was obviously back in work mode. Becky had a lot to think about. It felt good to have another woman on her side. Hell, it felt good to know the other camera operators were on her side and didn't think she was pathetic. She took a deep breath and headed toward the group. It was going to be a long day, but deep down inside Becky felt a spark of her old self returning. It was time to stop letting Marissa and the guys on the show make her feel bad.

✸

WHEN THE GROUP got back to the house it was time for another ceremony. Becky had been massaged and made up and poked within an inch of her life. She was tired and cranky and didn't feel like herself at all. They'd stuffed her into a designer dress with two inch heels. They'd wanted to put her in four inch heels, but Becky flat-out refused. There was no way she'd be able to walk in anything higher than the two inches she was currently wearing. Not only did her feet *already* hurt, but she just knew she'd fall on her face on national television if they made her wear the higher heels.

They'd teased her hair and put it up in a fancy upsweep and had caked makeup on her face. She'd never had so much on before in her life and she knew she probably looked ridiculous. She only wanted to go and take a shower, put on her stretchy pants and a T-shirt and get back to her normal self.

That night at the casual meet and greet time before the ceremony, the men all seemed to take extra notice of her. Becky knew it was a result of the spa treatment and not because they suddenly wanted to get to know her. All this crap she was wearing wasn't her. It was ridiculous that all of a sudden the men were paying more attention to her. She knew Dean hadn't been there when they'd gotten back. At least she hadn't seen him, but all of a sudden she felt a tingle up the back of her neck and knew he'd arrived.

She refused to turn around. She didn't want to see the same look in his eyes as in the men all around her. Well, she *did* want to see him looking at her admiringly, but she was scared he'd only look at her that way because of what they'd done to her, not because of who she was inside. She was afraid what he'd think about the new-and-improved her. Afraid that he'd like it too much, and afraid that he wouldn't like it at all. Gah! She was so confused and so stressed out.

Finally, after a long day and night, it was her turn to stand in front of the men and make her choices. Robert had done his normal speech and asked the women to choose who they wanted to stay. She still really didn't care who stayed and who left. For the first time Marissa hadn't tried to come to her before the show and tell her who to have stay. The touchy-feely, working together times were over.

Becky knew Marissa had already chosen her favorites, and asked that Trevon leave, so she chose the best of the bunch that was remaining. She actually felt bad she had to tell someone to leave, because she didn't really even know the men that were left. In another spurt of defiance toward Marissa she'd deliberately not chosen Conner, so he'd have to leave the show. She'd overheard Marissa telling him how much she liked him and couldn't wait to go on an individual date with him. Well, as much individual as you could get when you were essentially on a double date, date with him.

"The choice has been made!" Robert boomed once again. Becky felt good about the fact that she hadn't flinched that time. She'd finally been expecting the cheesy line.

When it was over and the cameras were shut down she turned to leave to go and shower when Eddie called her name and gestured for her to come and talk to him. She reluctantly went over to where he and Dean were standing. She'd almost forgotten Dean was there, almost.

"Becky, since you're one of the stars of the show I'd like for you to take some time and talk to Dean about your role in the show and your favorite parts," he told her gravely.

She knew what he was really saying. He wanted her to talk up the show and try to influence Dean to finance his next reality venture. He knew how she really felt, at least he *should* know how she really felt. With Eddie there was no telling. He was good at ignoring everyone around him and plowing ahead with whatever he wanted to do, damn the consequences. Eddie stood there expectantly, waiting for her to start talking. Awkward!!

"If you don't mind, Eddie, I'd like to talk to Becky alone. I think she'll be more honest if she doesn't have to worry about pleasing you." Dean put his hand on Becky's elbow and led her toward a set of chairs just off the set.

Eddie had no choice but to let them go. He was sucking up big time and he didn't want to do anything his future investor wouldn't like. He didn't go far, but at least he was out of earshot.

"How are you doing, sweetheart?" Dean asked in a

low voice, helping her to sit but never letting go of her arm.

Becky looked at Dean, thrilled they were getting a chance to talk, but also nervous as she wasn't sure where they stood now. She shivered as his fingers caressed her elbow covertly.

"I-I'm fine." She stumbled over her words, then continued, "Are you really going to invest in another reality show?" She couldn't help it, that just blurted out. Even with Jonathan telling her he wasn't really going to invest she had a hard time believing he'd go to the lengths he had just so he could see her. She didn't *really* believe he'd want to invest in something as silly as a reality show, but she didn't know him all that well. She wanted to hear the confirmation from his lips directly.

"Of course not!" Dean exclaimed. "Why would I invest in something as ridiculous as this kind of show? But it was the only way I could think of to be able to be close to you for the next few weeks." He winked as he said it.

Becky was flattered, but the day had taken a toll on her and her confidence, even with the pep talk she'd gotten from Kina and from herself.

"Why, Dean? I mean, it's not like you're hurting for women. Why work so hard for me? I'm nobody special," she finished honestly, looking him in the eye.

Dean turned his chair around so they were face to

face instead of side by side and leaned in close. Not too close so it'd be inappropriate to anyone who might be watching, but close enough he was looking her in the eyes and somehow talking straight to her heart.

"Becky, I told you last night, it's *you* I want to get to know. There's something about you, something true, something that speaks to me. I've never felt this way before and I want to see where it goes. And you're the most beautiful woman in this room and the most beautiful woman I've honestly ever seen."

Becky snorted. "Yeah right, Dean, give me a break! I've never been called beautiful by anyone before, and no matter how much makeup I'm wearing right now I know it's still not the case!" She was embarrassed at her outburst and dropped her eyes to the ground between them.

"Becky," Dean said urgently. "Please look at me." When she didn't look up, he continued, "I want to put my hand under your chin and raise your head so you have to look at me, but I know that would look strange to Eddie and other people. Please. Please look at me."

Becky raised her head and managed to meet his eyes. God, she was so courageous and beautiful to him. "It's not what you're wearing, or what you look like on the outside, although you *are* beautiful on the outside…it's who you are inside. You'd never tell anyone they were stupid, or not be a friend to someone based on the way they look. You appreciate animals and would do anything to help them. You'd rather wear sweats and be comfortable than put on heels and a fancy dress and hobnob with the most important people in the world. *That* is what I find beautiful about you. In fact..." he continued earnestly, "I much prefer you in your jeans and T-shirt than that dress and your hair done up and your face covered in gunk."

Becky giggled. He sure knew how to make her feel better. She saw he wasn't smiling back at her. He was serious as he could be. God, what she'd give to not be here, to be able to snuggle down into his arms and rest her head on his chest. To feel safe.

Dean tried to relax. God, he wanted to haul her over his lap and hold her close to his chest. He wanted to kiss the hell out of her so everyone around would know she was his. He wanted to mark her as his. He could just imagine how a hickey would look on her neck. Juvenile, but he couldn't help it. He couldn't stand it when the men on the show were ogling her before the ceremony. He was surprised at her looks when she got back from the spa, but he was being honest with her when he'd told her he preferred her other look. Done up the way she was now she just looked fake. She looked stiff and uncomfortable. He much preferred her in her natural state.

"Did Jonathan give you the phone?" he asked Becky,

scooting his chair back a bit and leaning back. If he didn't change the subject and put some space between them she'd end up in his lap no matter who was watching. He didn't want to give Eddie any reason to suspect he was anything other than an investor.

Becky nodded. "I'm not sure exactly why you gave it to me, though…especially if you're going to be around the set."

"I was hoping we could talk when you went up to your room at night. God, Becky," his voice got huskier, "I'd love to imagine you lying in your bed, wearing some sexy silky thing talking to me…" He cleared his throat and continued, "I also wanted you to know you had an ally, and a way to get in touch with the outside world if you needed it."

"Thank you," Becky said. "I'd enjoy talking to you and getting to know you as well." He might want to think about her lying in her bed, and she could almost picture it in her mind. Both of them lying on their backs lazily, talking about their day…crap, she had to concentrate. She couldn't go there right now, as much as she wanted to think about him naked in bed.

She tried to be funny. "First of all, I don't sleep in anything silky and sexy. Typically I sleep in boy shorts and a tank top."

Dean gulped. "Jesus, hon. You're going to give me a heart attack. Before I could only imagine what you'd look like in bed, but you've just given me a perfect picture that I won't be able to get out of my head."

Becky smiled shyly at him, enjoying knowing he'd be thinking about her in bed. Changing the subject, she said, "I don't think they'd kick me off the show if I got caught with the phone, but you never know, so we'd have to be careful." She watched as he nodded in agreement and then continued. "I'm not sure why I'd need to get in touch with the outside world as you called it, but thank you just the same. I appreciate it more than you know that someone is trying to look out for me."

"You're killing me, sweetheart," Dean said, compassion shining in his eyes. "I'll always look out for you."

The two smiled at each other, communicating without words. Dean knew his time was up for the night. He didn't want it to end, but he saw Eddie walking toward them.

"I'll see you tomorrow, Becky," he said softly. "I'll let you sleep tonight, but I'll call tomorrow night. You can tell me how your day went and all the things you'd tell a friend about this experience that you can't tell anyone else."

Becky could only nod and watch as he shook Eddie's hand and expressed delight in talking to her.

"When you come by next I'll let you spend some time with Marissa," Eddie told him excitedly. Becky frowned. It couldn't be helped, but she hoped Dean was telling the truth about all the things he'd said to her today. Becky knew Marissa would really lay on the charm just to prove she was more attractive to Dean than she was.

## Chapter Eight

THE NEXT NIGHT, Becky went up to bed exhausted. Marissa was going out of her way to be snide and rude and to try to make her look bad. Becky supposed it was a direct result of the way she'd stuck up for herself at the spa yesterday. It was hard to keep up a pretense of being happy and enjoying herself when all she had to deal with every day was fake people who were doing their best to make her miserable.

After her shower, Becky lay down on her bed and just stared at the ceiling. Seriously, why had she thought this would be a good idea? She'd probably lose whatever friends she did have when the show finally aired. She knew it wasn't going to show her in a good light and she was totally depressed. How could it? She couldn't hide from the cameras, they were everywhere. And while she remembered Kina had said all the camera people liked her, they still had to film her, it was their job.

She also remembered what Kina had said about that Australian show, how Sam was edited out after the first episode when in reality she didn't leave until at least half way through the show. If she was lucky, Eddie would do that to her as well. She could be edited out first thing and no one would have to see her be humiliated day in and day out. Becky sighed. She didn't think it would be possible, however, since the entire premise of the show was all the men "fighting over" two women bachelorettes.

Then today there was Dean. Specifically, watching Marissa suck up to him and put her hands all over him. Dean had come back to the show on Eddie's request and he'd introduced them, just as he had with Becky yesterday. Marissa had taken every chance she could to touch him. She patted his arm, she stood very close to him, and at one point she leaned in while laughing and put her hand on his chest. Becky wanted to march over to them and tear Marissa's hair out. It frankly surprised her as she generally wasn't a jealous woman, but there was just something about Dean that made her want to claim him as her own in front of the world. She sighed. She wasn't sure she was going to make it the last few weeks.

She could tell Dean was trying to put distance between him and Marissa as they spoke, but it just wasn't working. He looked at her a few times, but when Marissa realized what he was doing, she manipulated them so his back was to her and he couldn't see her anymore. Becky remembered Marissa's smirk at her when she did it too. What a bitch.

Becky lay there on her bed, enjoying the quiet. All she could hear was the tick-tock of the wall clock in her room. Suddenly she felt her pillow vibrating…what the heck? Then she remembered she'd put the phone under her pillow to hide it, and so it was close at hand…just in case, and it was ringing. She reached under her head and pulled it out and answered hesitantly…just in case it wasn't Dean.

"Hi, Becky," Dean said in a low smooth voice. "How are you?"

Becky was thrilled to hear from him. He called! Just like he said he would. She felt like she was back in the seventh grade and was giddy to be hearing from a boy. Becky was instantly awake. She scooted up the bed and rested her back against the headboard.

"Tired," Becky told him honestly. "It's getting harder and harder to stay up each night and pretend to like what I'm doing."

"I could tell," Dean told her. "I'm worried about you. You didn't eat much tonight."

Becky flushed, even though she knew he couldn't see her.

"Believe me, Dean, I eat enough…too much probably." She gave a short laugh.

"Please don't," Dean told her. "As I've already told

you, you're beautiful and perfect. I like you exactly the way you are. Don't let those people make you feel like you can't eat a normal meal. *They* are the ones who aren't normal!" he said urgently.

Becky sighed. She knew he was right. She *knew* it. "I know, but…" Her voice trailed off. "It's just hard." That was a lame explanation, and sort of like calling the ocean "big." She didn't really know how to explain it, but she tried. "I feel like I'm in this bubble. I'm floating around, watching what's going on around me. I can see the dangerous sharp things around that will pop my bubble and since I'm not steering, all I can do is hope I don't run into them. I'm always aware of the cameras and I can't help but think of when this show finally airs what it's going to make me look like. I know that sounds vain and selfish, but I'm trying to watch everything I say and everything I do and everywhere I look, but I know I'm still making a fool out of myself." Becky's voice trailed off once more.

Dean was furious, not at Becky, but at Eddie and the director. They were shredding this woman's self-esteem in front of his eyes, and he couldn't say or do anything to stop it. He felt as helpless as she just described being inside a floating bubble.

"Listen, Becky," he told her with urgency lacing his tone. "Please. This is what *I* saw today watching you…will you listen to me?"

Becky nodded, then realizing he couldn't see her, mumbled, "Uh-huh."

Dean took a deep breath. He knew this moment was very important and what he said to her now would hopefully lighten her load.

"During lunch today, when Marissa was complaining about the temperature of the soup, you touched the server's hand and thanked her for her efforts. You probably didn't know this, but she smiled all the way back to the kitchen simply because you took the time to compliment her. Out by the pool when everyone else was swimming and playing, you were sitting in the lounge chair. When everyone went in, you gathered up all of the used towels and put them on a chair so someone else didn't have to do it. You smiled at one of the camera operators for no special reason as you went into the house. I even saw you tell one of the assistant producers happy birthday, when no one else on the show seemed to care. Hell, I have no idea how you even knew it *was* his birthday! Even when the clueless men on the show are ignoring you and simpering all over Marissa, when they aren't able to get near her, you still talk to them and try to get to know them. You answer all their questions about Marissa and try to give them hope she just might choose them. I even saw you open a damn window today because a fly was buzzing on the pane and couldn't get outside. You're a good person,

Becky. To the core. No matter what these people throw at you, no matter what they say, you remember this…I see you. I see the real you. Not only do I see you, I like what I see. And I know America will see it too."

His voice tapered off. He waited. He heard Becky sniff once. Oh God, he'd made her cry. He hadn't meant to make her cry. "Sweetheart?" he asked softly. "I didn't say all that to make you cry." When she didn't immediately say anything, he said with frustration, "Damn, I should've kept my mouth shut. I want to be there to hold you, Becky, and it's pissing me off I can't be. Are you okay?"

"I know, I'm okay, Dean. Really. I just…" She paused and sniffed again. "I've just had a bad day and that was possibly the nicest thing anyone has ever said to me in my entire life."

Dean laughed and tried to lighten the mood. He wanted her to stop crying, he couldn't stand it. "If that was the nicest, then I'd better get to work trying to beat it!"

Becky laughed, as she was supposed to. "Tell me more about yourself, Dean," Becky asked. "I don't know that much about you, only that we have this crazy chemistry." She laughed some more.

Dean smiled. She didn't know the half of it. He was so glad she wasn't crying anymore, he'd tell her anything she wanted to know. He proceeded to tell her about his family and about his job, how he was in the security field. He talked about what he liked and what he disliked and as much other information as he could. He answered all of her questions.

Becky also told Dean about herself in return. About how she didn't like to cook, how she liked her job, but didn't love it. She confessed while she had a lot of people that she knew, she didn't have a lot of close friends. She admitted she loved Arizona. It was a big and open land. And so far, away from the set at least, people had been very friendly.

Becky realized they'd been talking for over two hours. Ugh, she knew it'd be hard to get up tomorrow, well, today. It was well past midnight. Talking with Dean was soothing and she'd practically forgotten about the stupid show she was on and the tension she was feeling a few short hours ago.

"Dean, it's late, and while I've loved talking to you, I have to get going."

"I know, sweetheart," Dean told her regretfully, "I need to go as well."

Becky tried to ignore how much she loved hearing him call her sweetheart in his low rumbly voice. She felt it deep in her heart and it felt so good. Becky hesitated and then said quietly, "I have a question for you, though…" She didn't know how he'd take it. Then she mentally shrugged and just asked, "I need some ideas for my dates."

She waited and hearing nothing but silence on the other end of the line said, "I didn't mean that like it sounded." She laughed nervously. "I mean I need help on what to do here on the show. Marissa and I take turns choosing the dates and it's my turn coming up and I don't know what we should do. I'm not from around here…and…" Her voice trailed off.

Dean laughed. "I understand, hon. For a second there I thought you wanted my help in a different area about your 'dates'." They both laughed.

"I have an idea and I think after what you told me when we were at Devil's Canyon you'll think it's a good one. As I told you before, my family operates a refuge center for animals, including coyotes."

He heard Becky's indrawn breath and continued, "It's more a rescue center for the coyotes that have gotten too close to people's homes and are in danger of being killed as a result. I thought maybe you might like to go there and see not only the coyotes, but meet some of my family as well," Dean finished. He couldn't believe how nervous he was. He'd never cared enough about a woman to bring her home to meet his entire family and friends. He knew they'd talked about it when they were on the trail at Devil's Canyon, but that was "someday." Someday was now here. Would Becky want to do that with him? In her typical style, she didn't keep him waiting for her answer.

"Are you kidding?" Becky exclaimed. "I'd *love* that! Oh, Dean, I can't wait to see the animals." Her voice trailed off when she thought about the coyote she saw while hiking. "Does that mean you'll have to hunt and find the coyote I saw at the Canyon for your refuge?" she asked, worriedly thinking about how odd the animal's behavior had been.

"I doubt it," Dean answering honestly. "As long as there aren't any reports of attacks on people or anyone's pets, that coyote is probably safe."

Dean made sure Becky knew what the refuge was called so she could pass the information along to Eddie in the morning.

While he would have gladly talked to her all night, he could hear she was fading fast.

"I'm going to let you go, sweetheart," he told her softly. "I've loved talking to you and getting to know you better. One of these nights we'll have to do a different kind of talking while we're both in bed." He paused. When he heard her indrawn breath he continued, "I'm looking forward to my family meeting you. They'll love you. Sleep well, love."

"Good night." He heard Becky say breathlessly.

"Good night," he answered back and clicked off the phone.

Becky was more than half asleep. She clicked off her

phone and leaned down to grab the phone charger. She plugged it in and shoved it under her bed so it was out of sight. She only dared charge the thing at night when there was no chance of anyone seeing it. She snuggled down into the covers. She felt good. She'd gone to bed feeling depressed, but talking with Dean raised her spirits and she was looking forward to seeing his family's sanctuary, even though she had to "officially" spend the day with a man other than Dean. The last thing she thought of as she drifted off to sleep was his low voice calling her "love" as he'd ended their call.

## Chapter Nine

✦

THE NEXT DAY, Dean went to the refuge to meet with his parents and he explained he'd met his *One*. His parents, Steve and Bethany, were beyond pleased. Dean knew his parents' story by heart. When his dad explained to him and Jonathan how they'd probably meet a woman one day and know immediately she was the one for them, he'd told them how he met their mom.

Steve was a firefighter and he'd been called to the scene of a bad car wreck. Upon arriving he found out Bethany was the person who'd witnessed the accident and had called for help. He took one look at her standing on the side of the road, arms wrapped around her waist, waiting for help to arrive, and knew she'd be his.

Dean knew his dad was lucky. He'd really only half believed him about the knowing when he met a woman that she'd be the *One* for him, but there was no mistaking his feelings when he first laid eyes on Becky sitting on that rock on the trail at Devil's Canyon.

He explained to his parents a bit about how Becky was on a reality dating show and the role of wealthy investor he'd taken on so he could keep an eye on her. He also had to explain he'd invited her, and the production crew, to their family refuge. He supposed he should've asked permission first, but he knew his dad would understand and would not only want to meet Becky, but would think it was a great idea as well.

Their animal refuge was a safe place for all types of animals, but they had a lot of coyotes on the property. It allowed them a safe place to run and live without worrying about humans. Having the reality show filming on the property would be annoying, but it'd certainly be good to get some publicity and hopefully be able to raise some money to help with its continued upkeep.

Steve agreed to talk to all of the employees at the refuge and explain what was going on. Dean wanted to make sure everyone knew Becky was his *One* and wanted his dad to explain the circumstances. He didn't want anyone to look down on Becky because she was on the show and "dating" someone else when she was supposed to be his. He was looking forward to seeing her interact with the coyotes and his family and friends.

✸

Becky explained what she wanted to do to Eddie and

really had to push him to accept. It seemed the producers wanted her to choose to take the group ice skating at a nearby mall. Becky had never been ice skating before and knew it'd be just another chance to make her look bad, so she stuck to her guns and told them she chose the animal refuge and if they denied her she'd walk off the show. She wasn't sure she really had the guts or legal leg to do it, but everyone knew at this point if she did, it would ruin the entire show. Ultimately, Becky knew it wasn't her threats that made Eddie cave, but more the fact he'd found out his potential investor's family owned the refuge. That made him agree to allowing the dates to be filmed there.

Later that day, after the selection process to find out which of the remaining men would be going on the dates with them, they headed over to the refuge. The twins Derek and David were going, as were Dexter and John. Becky didn't really care anymore who won the dates. It wasn't like any of the men really wanted to hang out with her. She really didn't care for Derek and David, though. They were a bit creepy to her, but of course Marissa thought they were, in her words, dreamy, and was thrilled they'd be on their outing.

Becky hadn't seen Dean on the set that day, but knew he'd be at the refuge when they arrived. He'd said that his family owned it, so she figured he'd be there as well. She looked around to see if Jonathan was one of the camera operators assigned to the outing and when she didn't see him, she assumed he'd be staying back at the production house. She was a little disappointed. She didn't really know Jonathan, but she liked what she knew about him. She had time to watch people in the house each day, partly because it was boring as hell just sitting around all the time, but also because no one cared much about what she did, especially if Marissa was around.

She'd watched as Jonathan would help the other camera operators move equipment around. He always did his part and never let anyone struggle with anything on their own. He volunteered for the shifts she knew others didn't like. She'd even noticed him watching Kina with an interested look in his eye, but she never saw them actually talking.

Becky turned her attention back to the refuge they were approaching. As they neared the gate, Becky could see a ten foot high fence stretching as far as her eye could see. It lined the road and disappeared off into the distance. The property was huge and it looked like a wonderful place for coyotes and other animals to spend out their lives. She didn't know a lot about coyotes, but what she did know, fascinated her.

They pulled up to a huge house with a large white porch that surrounded the entire front of the building. There was a big red barn off to the side and a series of gates leading into the enclosure. Becky saw a man and a woman standing on the porch, obviously waiting for them. As they all stumbled out of the vans and the camera operators started setting up their equipment, she saw Eddie and the director walk over to the couple on the porch.

It wasn't long before they all came over to where she and Marissa were standing with their dates. Eddie introduced the couple as Steve and Bethany. Marissa shook their hands, but was obviously not interested much in them, she was too engrossed in her dates and Becky's dates and trying to keep hold of all of their interests.

In direct opposition to the way Marissa had acted when meeting the couple, Becky shook both Steve and Bethany's hands and expressed delight they'd allowed them to come to their refuge.

"It's our pleasure, Becky," Bethany said, holding on to Becky's hand a bit longer than was socially acceptable. Becky dropped her eyes at the intense gaze of the woman. It wasn't disrespectful, but Becky thought it best she didn't hold her eyes. She wasn't sure why, but it felt like the right thing to do. Bethany nodded, beamed, and dropped Becky's hand.

She squeezed her husband's hand in approval.

"We need to discuss a bit more with Eddie about the plans for the shoot today and what exactly we'll be doing. Please," Steve said, gesturing to the property, "look around, but don't go inside the gates, for obvious reasons, or the barn. We'll give you an official tour later."

They all nodded their heads. Marissa and her dates walked toward the production truck, intending to sit inside until shooting was ready to begin. Becky turned to Dexter and John, her dates for the day, and asked if they'd like to walk around. They looked back at Marissa, engrossed in conversation with David and Derek, shrugged their shoulders and agreed. The three of them, with a camera following, wandered over to the fence line near the barn. She didn't really want to spend time with the two men, but she figured since it was expected of her, she'd better at least try to look like she was enjoying the show. Better ratings and all that.

"I wonder if we'll see any of the coyotes today," Becky mused, straining her eyes to see any movement on the other side of the fence. There was a large pasture around the house, then a line of trees and a wood line. The coyotes were probably off in the woods doing whatever it was that coyotes did, but she sure hoped they'd get to see some of them.

The men finally got bored with her inane conversation and wandered off to the production truck where Marissa was holding court with the other men. Becky didn't care. She'd stay right where she was in the hopes of a glimpse of a coyote. She resisted the urge to look around for Dean. If he was there, he was there, but she didn't want to seem desperate to see him.

Dean found her about ten minutes later. She was sitting on the ground, legs crossed, with her elbows resting on her knees, her chin in her hands, scanning the countryside. He smiled. He was so in love with her. Hell, he had no idea why or how he'd fallen so fast, but there it was. Just looking at her made his heart beat faster and made him want to protect her from any and all threats. He never wanted her to be hurt. Ever.

He'd never understood how his dad and granddad fell in love so fast when they found their *One*, but now he knew. It was just there. That feeling of rightness and contentedness, and yes, love.

Dean walked over to Becky with his dad following close behind. He knew he wanted his father to approve of his woman. This was a big moment for him. He'd never wanted anything so badly in all of his life than for his dad to meet and like Becky. He didn't think it'd be a problem, but there was always that doubt. If they didn't like or approve of her it'd make coming home awkward. He loved his family and hoped they'd love Becky and vice versa.

Becky stood up when she saw the men coming toward her. She wiped her hands on her jeans and tried to knock off any stray grass or dirt she'd picked up by sitting on the ground. She hoped she wasn't doing anything wrong. She hadn't gone near the barn, but she couldn't read the expression on either one of their faces.

At seeing the nervous look Becky had on her face there was nothing more that Dean wanted to do than to sweep his woman up in a huge reassuring hug, but he knew he had to show some decorum, especially with all the production crew hanging around, not to mention the director and Eddie as well.

"Hi, Dean," Becky said shyly as they walked up to her.

Dean reached over, took her hand and squeezed it tightly in his.

"I know you met my parents earlier, but I wanted to introduce you myself." He turned to Steve and dipped in a formal little bow. "Steve, this is Becky." Then he turned toward Becky. "Becky, this is Steve."

Becky didn't know why Dean was being so formal in introducing her to his dad, but she unconsciously mirrored Dean's motions and bowed a bit when she took his dad's hand. She knew somehow this was an important moment, but she wasn't sure why or how. All she knew was that she hoped Steve liked her since he was Dean's father and it seemed so important to him.

"It's very nice to meet you, Mr. Baker, and I'm so thankful you let us all come out today. I know it's terribly intrusive for all the cameras and such, and I'm sure you'll be bored to tears once they actually do start filming. Your place is beautiful and the animals are so lucky to be able to call this home and be safe here."

She looked up at Dean's dad and watched him smile at her.

"You're right, Becky, they're lucky, but we're lucky too. We get to watch them get healthy and know they're safe for the rest of their lives. And please know that as Dean's girlfriend you're welcome here anytime. You come back with Dean after the show is over and we'll have dinner…okay? But I only have one condition." He paused for dramatic affect and continued quickly when he saw Dean frown. "You have to call me Steve, not Mr. Baker."

They all laughed and Becky readily agreed.

Dean smiled as his dad slapped him good naturedly on the back.

"Thank you, Dad…just…thank you," he told him sincerely, not quite able to hold back the emotion in his voice. His dad seemed to like Becky. All would be right in their world as soon as the damn reality show was over.

As the tension seemed to be over, Becky couldn't hold her excitement back anymore and blurted out, "Where are all the animals? Will we get to see them today?"

Dean and his dad chuckled together.

"Patience, little one," Steve told her. "They'll come. You'll see lots of animals today."

Just then they heard Eddie call for attention over a bullhorn and proclaim they'd start shooting in twenty minutes.

"I'd better go," Becky said, looking over her shoulder at the group gathering near the production truck. "Seriously…" she said nervously, "this is going to be really boring…you don't want to watch, do you?"

She hoped he wouldn't, that no one else would have to watch her in this stupid show and see her be humiliated.

"It's okay, sweetheart," Dean told her soothingly. "Remember what I told you yesterday."

Becky sighed. "Okay, well…thanks again, Steve. It was so nice to meet you. You've undertaken something of great importance here and I'll try to make sure it gets across on the show." She turned around and walked toward the others.

Steve looked at his son. "I like her, Dean, I like her a lot."

Dean grinned. "So do I, Dad, so do I!"

✴

THE SHOW GOT started about forty minutes later. They were supposed to walk around the fence toward the barn. Then once they got in the barn, they were supposed to be shown how the food was prepared. Once that was wrapped up they'd be given a chance to feed some of the animals, including the coyotes. They were reassured that the coyotes knew the sound of the dinner bell, for lack of a better term for it, and would show up for the food.

From the moment the cameras started Marissa became lively and energetic…and claimed the spotlight. She exclaimed how beautiful the refuge was and wondered if the coyotes would be scary…and Becky knew what was to come. When they did finally see them she'd play the damsel in distress and get all the men to reassure her that she was safe.

For once Becky didn't care what Marissa did, she was just so happy to be here at all. This really was a chance of a lifetime. She hadn't lied when she'd told Dean it was her dream to own a place like this. She'd always loved animals and it'd be such a privilege to be able to help them when they needed it.

Becky listened as their guide, Sarah, took them around and explained the process of how the various animals came to be at the refuge and what they did once they were here. She talked about the horses that were abused and neglected, she told stories about some of the dogs and cats and how they ended up with them. She even explained how coyotes don't necessarily mate for life like wolves do, but that the mated pair would usually stay together for a number of years before they went their separate ways.

The refuge even had some cubs born on the property in the past as well. Sarah explained how they prepared the food and how they even had some live food out in the boundary as well. They didn't want the coyotes to be bored or get too used to people, which could happen if they were always fed prepared slabs of meat. There were plenty of squirrels, mice, birds, snakes and other live animals they could feed on.

"Are you ever scared of the coyotes or other animals?" Marissa interrupted, not being able to stand not being the center of attention.

"Not really," answered Sarah. "We learn to read them pretty well and know the signs if they are feeling aggressive and when we should avoid them."

"Do you go into the pen?" asked Becky, unable to keep her questions to herself anymore.

Sarah smiled at Becky. She knew all about Becky and how she was Dean's woman, even if Becky herself didn't know it yet. It was good she was showing interest and asking questions since she'd be in the family soon.

"We do," she answered. "You have to understand, these are wild coyotes, but some have been here a while and do recognize us. They are *not* domestic dogs, as some people like to think, but they're also not aggressive killing machines as others believe either."

Becky smiled and the little group continued walking around, observing some of the other animals and generally getting a tour of the property. As soon as they walked into the barn Marissa couldn't stop complaining about the smell. She'd pretended to gag and covered her nose and mouth with her hand.

David happened to have a handkerchief with him and gave it to her. Becky thought it was extremely rude. The barn smelled like…well, a barn. Becky thought to herself that Marissa was born to be melodramatic.

Sarah rang the bell that hung outside the back of the barn and soon Becky saw shapes running toward them from the tree line.

"Oh my gosh," she said quietly, "they're beautiful."

Ten coyotes came running to the fence. They were different shapes and sizes and even ages. They did look a lot like dogs. Becky couldn't take her eyes off of them. She stepped up to the fence and grasped the chain link and just stared. She didn't notice the crowd of people off to the side. Many of the employees at the refuge wanted to meet the woman Dean had claimed, and even more so because she was on a television show.

They weren't sure what to think, especially after seeing how Marissa acted with the men and her attitude toward all of them. The employees all hoped Becky was good enough for their employer's son. They all relieved to hear Steve approved of her, but they also wanted to see for themselves.

"Would you like to feed them?" Sarah asked the group.

"Ick!" Marissa immediately said disgustingly. "No way!"

The men agreed, which was no surprise, they wouldn't disagree with anything Marissa said.

Sarah looked expectantly at Becky.

"I'd love to," Becky said quietly. "Will they let me? I mean, they don't know me."

Sarah nodded. "I'll be right next to you, it'll be fine."

Marissa and her dates, at least that was how Becky thought of the men at this point, sat on a set of bleachers nearby. They were set up for demonstrations such as this one when groups came to the refuge. Marissa was between her dates and not paying any attention to the coyotes or anything Becky was doing. She'd turn from one man to another, flirting with all of them, trying to hold all of their attentions.

Becky followed Sarah into the pen, oblivious to the crowd of people. She'd gotten so used to so many people being around the shoot that she tended to just ignore them all. Dean stood with his mom and dad along with some of the other employees and watched the interaction between Sarah, his woman, and the coyotes.

Becky watched carefully how Sarah threw the meat toward the group of coyotes, then stepped back. When it was time, Sarah told her to go ahead and throw the meat toward the coyotes. Becky threw it exactly where Sarah told her to aim.

The coyotes basically ignored the humans and feasted on their meal. Becky noticed a small coyote slinking toward the others. She hadn't noticed it before. It was smaller than the others and hesitant. Becky asked Sarah about it.

"Oh, that's our newest arrival," Sarah told her. "We don't know her story yet, but we think she was a part of a traveling zoo. She was kept in a small box and beaten by the humans who kept her locked up. Eventually the zoo was raided by the humane society and the cops and she was freed. We were contacted and she came here to live. She doesn't trust us, and she doesn't trust the other coyotes in the sanctuary yet either. We aren't sure what to do about her. If she's not accepted by the other coyotes then we can't leave her here. They'll turn against her and she'll be worse off than she was before."

Becky thought that was the saddest thing she'd ever heard. For an animal to live through all that abuse and then not be accepted into the group of coyotes here at the refuge was just so awful.

"How long has she been here?" Becky asked, not taking her eyes off the coyote.

"For about two weeks," Sarah told her.

Becky gasped. "Has she eaten at all since she's arrived?" It certainly didn't look like it as the coyote was very skinny.

"I'm not sure," Sarah answered honestly. "She might be catching some of the small rodents and animals that are around their penned in area, but we have no way of knowing for sure."

Sarah knew she and the other employees at the refuge had tried everything they could to get the coyote to trust them. They'd tried to approach her, but the animal was so scared that she wouldn't let them anywhere near her. They'd even thrown the food so it would land right in front of her, but she always ignored it and another one of the coyotes ended up eating it instead. Sarah had told Becky the truth. They weren't sure what to do with the little coyote. It was breaking their hearts, but if she couldn't bond with them or the other coyotes, she'd have to go elsewhere for her own safety.

Becky continued to look at the little coyote. She could see she was scared to death, and had only come near the other animals and the fence because she was probably starving. Becky couldn't stand it anymore.

"Do you think I could try to feed her?" she asked Sarah. Sarah looked at Dean's woman. The match couldn't have been more perfect. Sarah knew Dean liked to protect people and even made a career out of it.

Becky was trying to protect the little coyote as best she knew how. Sarah thought she'd do Steve's family proud. She didn't think she'd be successful with the little coyote, but it wouldn't hurt for her to try.

"Of course you can, Becky, just don't feel bad if she won't come near you or if she won't eat."

Sarah went over with her again about the proper way to feed a coyote and what to do. She didn't think Becky was really listening to her, though, and finally just told her to go ahead.

Becky didn't know what she was doing. She only knew that if she didn't try to help this little coyote she'd regret it forever. The animal didn't deserve to be in a traveling zoo. She didn't deserve to go through her life rejected and not trusting. Becky watched the coyote flinch when Marissa's shrill laugh suddenly sounded loud in the clearing. She took her eyes off the enclosure long enough to glare at the woman, only to see Steve striding over to the woman and her dates. Thank God. Steve would take care of her and make her shut up.

After entering the fenced-in area Becky walked about forty feet away from the feeding area. Far enough away that she'd be in big trouble if the coyotes decided they wanted to eat *her*, but she didn't care. She was focused on the little scared coyote. She thought it'd be best to get it away from the humans, the barn, and the other animals. She sat down cross-legged with her back to the barn and the people. Becky knew they were all still there, watching her, but she didn't care, she was solely focused on the sad little animal in front of her.

She sat very still, with her head down but had her eyes up, watching the little coyote. She held the small piece of meat in her hand, outstretched on the ground in front of her. And she waited. For ten minutes the coyote didn't move. She didn't move toward her, but she also didn't run away either. Becky decided to be encouraged by that rather than discouraged. The other coyotes finished eating and, taking a wide berth around her, headed back toward the wood line, and still she and the coyote sat still, waiting each other out.

Becky sat very still. Her legs were asleep, but she didn't move. Finally, after what seemed an eternity, the small coyote took one step toward her and then sat again. That one step lifted Becky's spirits immensely. She'd sit out there all day if that was what it took. Becky decided to start talking to the coyote. She spoke low and quietly. She crooned nonsense to her. She told her how pretty she was and how she didn't blame her for not trusting people. She told the little coyote that it wasn't her fault. That if she trusted these people they'd help her. That this was a safe place, one where she could heal and grow big and strong. She continued to murmur nonsense to the coyote in the hopes the animal would hear the lack of anger and encouragement in her voice.

Dean's family and friends watched silently from nearby. They were standing close enough that they could hear everything Becky was murmuring to the little coyote. They held their breaths. They wanted Becky to succeed just as much as she herself did. When the little coyote took another step toward her they were amazed.

One employee whispered, "She's gonna do it." Everyone else just nodded in agreement and held their breaths. They all felt humbled watching Becky charm the little coyote and get her to trust again.

Becky held her breath as well. This was it. The little coyote was only about four feet from her. Sweat ran down the side of Becky's face, but she ignored it.

"Okay, little one. I'm going to throw this meat toward you…don't be scared, okay? Here it comes." Becky gave the meat a light toss and it landed right in front of the coyote. At first the animal backed up, but suddenly she shot forward, snatched up the meat, and backed up about ten feet and stared at Becky.

"Go ahead, it's okay," Becky soothed, her voice quivering with excitement. "It's all yours. You just go ahead and eat it. These people are here to help you. They won't hurt you. You have to trust them. They only want you to get better."

She watched as the little coyote gulped down the meat. Then instead of running off, the coyote sat there and stared at Becky expectantly.

"I'm sorry, I don't have any more," Becky told the coyote sadly, holding her empty hands out.

She held out her hand toward the coyote. "Come here," she coaxed, not knowing what she was doing. Was she even supposed to be touching a wild coyote? Should she be trying to touch a wild animal that was abused? She figured probably not, but this coyote needed some sort of comforting touch. She'd probably never experienced such a thing before, not even from another of her kind.

"Come on," she said again, wiggling her fingers, half wondering if she'd lose them. Becky didn't hear Sarah or anyone else complaining or freaking out, so she continued to try to coax the coyote toward her. As slowly as before, the coyote made her way toward Becky. Finally, when she was about two feet from her, she dropped to her haunches and crawled toward her outstretched hand.

The first time her hand touched the top of the little coyote's head, Becky fell in love. Her coat was rough and coarse. It was also matted and dirty, but the head under the fur was so tiny and delicate. Becky knew this coyote would be gorgeous once cleaned up and given some love.

"Come on, come here," she continued to coax. Slowly, ever so slowly, the little coyote crawled closer to Becky until her head was in Becky's lap. Becky stroked her head and shoulders, murmuring the whole time what a good girl she was and how pretty she was.

Dean looked over at his mom and saw tears streaming down her face.

Bethany turned toward her son and said, "Do you know how many of us have tried to do what your woman has just done? We tried everything, but that little coyote wouldn't come near us. We're so fortunate she came by today and we're so happy for you."

Dean beamed, but said with caution, "She doesn't know she's mine yet, mom. She has no idea how I feel or about our family history with the *One* and all that."

Bethany scolded him with her eyes. "Look at her, Dean, does that look like a woman who'll freak out when you tell her?"

Dean chuckled. "No, but I also don't want to scare her away just yet."

"Take your time, son. She's yours and you have plenty of time to get her used to the idea. Just don't wait too long. It's obvious this place needs her."

They looked back toward Becky just in time to see the little coyote stand up and push Becky over. Dean was about to burst into the pen and save Becky from a mauling when they heard her laugh. The little coyote was actually playing with her!

Becky giggled as the coyote pushed her over. She was so happy she thought she'd bust. This moment would be forever etched in her memory as one of the best experiences of her life. She looked over toward the crowd of people standing by the barn and caught Dean's eye. He was beaming at her and she felt tingles go down to the tips of her toes.

"Ewwww…look! She rolled in crap!" Marissa screeched, pointing at Becky.

Sure enough Becky had fallen backward when she'd been tackled by the coyote and had gotten some manure in her hair. She heard the men laughing along with Marissa. She couldn't hear what they were saying, but she immediately felt embarrassed and humiliated.

The little coyote had immediately jumped off of Becky at Marissa's loud words and was walking backward, growling. The moment was broken. Once again Marissa had brought all the attention back to her and made Becky look like a fool.

Becky watched sadly as the little coyote turned and bounded away toward the woods without looking back. She slowly stood up, painfully aware, now, of what she looked like. Her jeans were dirty, her hands and shirt smelled like something rotten from coming in contact with the filthy coyote, and she had poop in her hair. Great, just great. She could just imagine the camera angles on this one.

Becky walked back toward Sarah and the barn with a fake smile on her face. Of course her humiliation had to be witnessed by not only Dean, but his friends, family, and the cameras—and thus the world. She ducked her head. If only she could get away for a moment to compose herself. She wanted to cry.

As soon as she got back to the gate where Sarah was waiting to let her out of the pen, the cameras were right there. Eddie had decided while she was in the pen with the little coyote that this would make a great backdrop for the next ceremony. He was also probably trying to show off to Dean and impress him so he'd decide to invest in him. He'd ordered the cameras to capture Becky in all her gloriousness while ordering another producer to head back to the house and gather the other contestants and Robert so they could join them at the refuge for a ceremony.

Becky was horrified. Was he serious? As if it wasn't bad enough she'd just been humiliated by Marissa on national television, now he wanted to bring all the other men here to witness it? Jesus. Eddie must hate her. Becky felt her face heat up. She held her head up and took a deep breath. Fine. So be it.

She tried to ignore the camera as she went through the gate to the yard. She thought she saw Kina, if she remembered the camera operator's name right, in an argument with Eddie off to the side, but turned away, knowing she had to watch where she was walking or else she'd fall on her face.

She knew by Eddie deciding to have the ceremony immediately she wouldn't be able to do anything about her appearance. He wanted her to look like she was, the jerk. She looked around and grabbed a piece of twine off the ground that was used to bale hay and tied her hair up with it. She might have crap in her hair, but at least she could tie it up so it wasn't as obvious.

Becky refused to look at Dean or his family again. Sarah came over and touched her arm.

"Hey Becky," she said, "You did good, *really* good. I couldn't believe it when she came over to you! That was amazing."

Becky smiled at the woman. It *was* amazing, and she was proud of herself, but she knew she'd have to get through the next hour or so before she could let herself think about it again. She'd have to be on her guard against the snide comments she was sure she'd receive.

"Thanks Sarah," she said in a tight voice and walked away, not looking back.

Sarah growled under her breath and took a step toward Becky's retreating back. Dean suddenly appeared at Sarah's side, grabbing her elbow before she could take off after Becky.

"Let her be," he said intensely.

Sarah shook her head. "Let me go, Dean, I'm going to go shove that other woman's head in the dirt."

Dean gripped her arm harder, but not hurtfully,

knowing the longtime employee and friend would do just that given half a chance.

"That will humiliate Becky even more," he said simply, somehow knowing it was true.

It was the right thing to say. Dean could feel Sarah's body relax.

"Bitch!" she said about Marissa to no one in particular.

Then she turned toward Dean again, "Oh my God, Dean, did you see that? She…was…awesome…*that* was awesome."

Dean smiled and nodded, gazing toward Becky. "She *is* awesome, Sarah. Awesome."

✹

BECKY GRITTED HER teeth throughout the next hour. She had to endure the comments and joking from the rest of the men once they'd arrived at the refuge. They hadn't seen the miracle of the little coyote, they only saw her covered in dirt and smelling like shit, literally. She didn't need them making sarcastic comments about the 'smell in the air.' Becky knew she smelled, she could smell herself.

Marissa, of course, took the opportunity to tell everyone how Becky had rolled in crap in the yard and how funny she'd looked. She, of course, didn't mention anything about the coyote and what had happened.

Becky tried to tell one group of the men, but their attention was quickly diverted by Marissa's wild laughter nearby. Their heads turned and Becky lost their attention. Becky gave up. She didn't have an ally on the show. She figured at least Steve and Bethany were happy, but since they weren't on the show it didn't help her at the moment.

The ceremony was the same as usual. Marissa and Becky had to choose the men who they wanted to stay and who they wanted to leave. Becky barely cared about any of them. They were all out to get fame and fortune by winning Marissa's hand…and hers too if that was what they had to do. It wasn't like they actually wanted to be picked by *her*, but they'd take it if it was the only option. They put on a good show during the ceremony, but generally she knew, as did everyone, that Marissa was the grand prize.

Marissa chose the men she wanted to stay and Becky did the same. When it was all over, Ryan and Samuel were going home.

"The choice has been made!" Becky couldn't even smile at Robert's theatrical antics anymore.

There were only seven men left. The twins, Derek and David, Jose, Patrick, James, Dexter, and John. They were all good looking, but also extremely shallow and fake.

## Chapter Ten

✦

AFTER WATCHING RYAN AND SAMUEL get into the limo that would take them away from the show for good, the day was finally over. Becky stood off to the side near the pen, looking out at the land, wondering if the coyotes were out there watching. She heard Marissa and some of the men complaining to Eddie about how she smelled and how they refused to ride in the same vehicle as her. She supposed she couldn't blame them, she did smell gross. She gripped the fence tighter, wishing she was at home, wishing…oh she didn't know anymore. She went from feeling great being around Dean, to feeling totally depressed after filming. She knew it wasn't healthy, but wasn't sure what do to about it either. A lone tear escaped before she could will it away. God, would this torture ever end? She'd never complain about her boring insurance job again.

Finally, after getting control of her tears and wiping her face, she turned around to go back toward the vehicles and saw Steve talking with Eddie. Eddie shook his hand, looked relieved and turned toward Marissa, Robert, and the other men and motioned for them to board the van.

Becky walked toward the group and took a deep breath, readying herself to bear the jokes and comments from the others with dignity, but was intercepted by Steve who took her firmly by the arm as she passed him.

"We're taking you home later, Becky," he told her, steering her away from the production vans and toward the house.

"But…" Becky said, craning her neck to look back at the van and the people loading themselves into it.

"I just talked to Eddie, and he agreed it'd be best if you cleaned up here and we took you back in a bit." Becky blushed a fiery red and looked down at her feet as he continued to guide them toward the house. Great. Just great. Now her humiliation was complete.

Steve suddenly stopped walking, took Becky by the shoulders and turned her toward him. He put his knuckle under her chin and forced her head up to look at him.

"Don't let that asshole get you down, Becky," he told her sternly. "Look around. Look at my friends and *your* friends now. Look how happy they are. *You've* done that. *You* have made us all very happy by doing something none of us were able to. We want to celebrate with you and we know if you go back now, you certainly won't get to celebrate. Do you want to stay? I can tell Eddie that you want to go back now..." He let his voice trail off, letting her think about what she wanted.

Becky did take a look around. The men and women that had been there today were all standing around talking to each other, smiling and laughing. They seemed happy. She was being selfish and conceited to think they were all looking at her and laughing.

She nodded shyly at Steve. "Thank you, Steve. I'd love to stay."

Steve nodded and turned toward the house with her elbow in his hand.

"Do you think, however," she started to ask hesitantly, "that I might be able to clean up before we celebrate?"

Steve laughed and nodded as he towed her toward the house.

Dean grabbed Becky as soon as she stepped into the house, away from the eyes of the production crew and the other contestants. He hugged her to him as tight as he dared.

Becky laughed and pushed frantically at Dean. "Let me go, Dean!" She laughed. "I smell horrible…you'll get it on you."

Dean released his hold on Becky enough to put a bit of room between them, but didn't let her go.

"You're amazing," he told her with a smile on his

face.

"No, you mean I'm smelly." She laughed back at him, deciding once and for all to shake herself out of the doldrums. "Seriously, let me go, I'm gonna get you all gross."

"You could never get me 'all gross'," he told her with a flare of heat in his eyes.

Just as he was bending down toward her to kiss the daylights out of her, they were surrounded by many of the people that had watched the entire incident with the little coyote, all talking at once.

"How did you do that?"

"That was awesome."

"That made my day."

"What a bitch that other woman is."

The comments flowed over her and she stared into Dean's gaze which had never left hers. She shut her eyes for a moment. It felt so good to finally be with people who were as thrilled with what had happened as she was.

She opened her eyes again only to find Dean still staring at her. She broke eye contact and said to the group in general, "Wasn't that cool?"

Everyone laughed with her. "*Now*, can I *please* go and clean up?" Everyone broke into uncontrolled laugher again and Bethany had to forcefully break through the circle of people surrounding her son and his *One*.

"Come on, Becky, I'm sure I can find you something to wear while we wash your clothes."

Becky smiled shyly at Dean's mom and nodded. She glanced back at Dean before disappearing into the bowels of the house.

Dean watched Becky walk away with his mom. His heart felt so big. Not only did Becky get along with his family, but she'd made a great impression on them as well. He'd wanted, like he had so many times before, to sweep her away from the set and protect her from the humiliation they were forcing on her, but he knew he couldn't. All he could do was support her at night when they talked and give her some great experiences with his family and friends, like today. Time would have to take care of the rest. Once she was away from the show and living a normal life, things would settle down.

When Becky came back down with Bethany she was wearing a pair of sweat pants and a T-shirt, probably one of Steve's. She smelled fresh and clean as if she'd just taken a shower. Hell, of course she had. Her hair was wet and was down around her shoulders. Dean had to force himself not to rush over to her and kiss the hell out of her. This was not the time nor the place to start something they couldn't finish.

Becky smiled at Dean shyly. "I hope this is okay. It was what I was most comfortable in."

Dean smiled. "Of course, sweetheart. Whatever you

want to wear is fine by me." He met his mom's eyes over Becky's shoulder and they smiled at each other.

All during dinner everyone re-hashed what happened that day. Becky learned more about what the little coyote had gone through before she'd gotten to the refuge and how indignant everyone was about it. They'd so wanted to help her and were losing hope that they could. Becky didn't understand why *she* was the one who was able to break through the little coyote's barrier, but she was so happy she had.

"Do you think she'll eat more now? That she'll trust you guys?" Becky asked worriedly.

Steve answered for the group. "I think so. We'll let Dean try to feed her next. I think maybe if you go out to the pen with him one more time tonight and she sees you with him maybe she'll learn to trust more than just you. And if your scent is on him, and vice versa, it'll give her an extra incentive."

Becky looked at Steve and then back at Dean. "My scent?"

Dean took her hand and explained. "Yeah, when I hold your hand, some of your skin cells get mixed in with mine." He rubbed his thumb back and forth over the back of her hand as he spoke. "The natural scent of your skin will mix with mine. A coyote's sense of smell is very strong and she'll be able to smell both of us, even after we're gone. It's worth a shot."

Becky nodded. "Great, let's go now!"

Everyone laughed. "In a bit, sweetheart, finish your dinner first," Dean told her, laughing at her enthusiasm while continuing to stroke her hand with his, not letting go, forcing her to finish her meal with her other hand.

Dean knew it was getting late and Becky would have to get back to the production set soon. He hated to leave her. He felt anxious when he was separated from her. He wished he knew if she was feeling the same intense feelings he was, but Dean knew he'd have to take their relationship slow at first and rely on her instincts to recognize him as her soul mate.

After eating, Dean excused himself and Becky so they could go back out to the pen to see if they could get the little coyote to come back and if she'd take food from Dean. He smiled at the knowing smile his parents gave him as he left the house. They knew he'd take advantage of the alone time with Becky to further his persuit of her as his own.

The two went out to the edge of the yard near the pen. Nobody followed them outside, knowing if they all went outside at the same time, they'd spook the little coyote. Dean grasped Becky's hand in his and led them to the fence. Once they arrived, he turned Becky so her back was to him and he curled his arms around her waist and pulled her back against him. They both sighed in contentment. They stood like that for a bit and finally Becky broke the silence.

"How is she going to know we're here?" Becky asked quietly.

"She'll know," Dean responded, leaning down and whispering directly into her ear, "but you can call to her if you want."

Becky turned her head and looked back at him with her eyebrows scrunched up in confusion.

"Just start out with a little howl, then make a little yipping noise…it doesn't have to be loud, just choose a pitch that you're comfortable with and see if it works. Yipping is how coyotes usually 'talk' to each other," Dean explained, laughing at the look on her face.

"I'm embarrassed," Becky said, ducking her head quickly and looking straight ahead again. "It's not the kind of thing a woman would normally do around a hot guy," she finished quickly, blushing.

Dean smiled and moved one hand away from her waist to grasp her chin lightly. He gently turned it back and up so he could look her in the eyes. "Sweetheart, don't you know? Nothing you'd do around me would turn me off. I'm already yours."

Becky stared at Dean, watching as he bent down toward her slowly. Her heart hammered in her chest. This was it! He was really going to kiss her! She'd dreamed about this moment for so long and now that it was here it felt as natural as breathing. She met him halfway, coming up on her toes. Their lips met and Becky swore she could feel sparks arc between them. She felt Dean's tongue swipe along the seam of her lips and she eagerly opened for him.

Dean groaned low in his throat. He was finally kissing his *One*. For real kissing her. He'd kissed her before when he'd dropped her off at the house after bringing her home from Devil's Canyon, but this was a *kiss*. She tasted amazing, like…Becky. He'd never kiss another woman as long as he lived. This was it for him. *She* was it for him.

He turned her in his arms without breaking the kiss. He wound his arms tightly around her back and pulled her close to his chest. Becky gasped and went right on kissing Dean. He was amazing. She almost felt lightheaded. His tongue swept around her mouth like he owned it. She loved every second. She met his tongue with her own and they took turns exploring each other's mouths.

Finally, giving her bottom lip a nip, Dean pulled back to let her take a breath, but kissed his way down her neck toward her shoulder. The T-shirt she was wearing was big on her and Dean easily swept aside the collar to suck and nibble on her shoulder. Goose bumps rose on Becky's flesh. Her head dropped back. She never wanted him to stop.

Dean's hands wandered of their own volition. He'd

been so patient with her, and himself, and he couldn't help it. He grazed his hands up Becky's sides until they were just under her breasts. He stopped his movement, but squeezed lightly. He felt her shiver and fought with himself to back off.

Dean didn't want to stop, but he knew he had to. First, his parents weren't more than a hundred yards away and secondly, he knew if he didn't stop now, he'd probably go further than Becky would be comfortable with. That was what ultimately made him curb his own reactions to her. He never wanted Becky to regret anything they did, and he didn't want to rush her.

He was going to have to take a long run tonight to get himself back under control. Becky finally noticed Dean had stopped nibbling on her neck. She slowly opened her eyes, only to look right into Dean's smiling face. One hand rubbed circles on her lower back while the other was still against her side and she could feel his thumb rubbing rhythmically on the soft fleshy underside of her breast.

She blushed like a virgin. "That was…er…" Her voice faded off.

Dean took up where she left off, "…amazing, wonderful, life changing," he whispered. Becky could only nod and bury her face into Dean's shoulder. She felt him rest his chin on the top of her head and was grateful he was giving her time to control herself.

Finally, she took a deep breath and looked up at him with a shy smile. "Just make a few yipping sounds and the coyote will come, huh?" she said shakily, changing to a more neutral subject. Even though she wanted nothing more than for Dean to lay her down right there in the dirt and make love to her, she knew they couldn't do it. She wanted him so badly, but felt like they needed to get to know each other better before taking their relationship to that level. She respected him even more for not even trying to go any further than they already had.

Dean turned her in his arms so her back was once again nestled against his chest and wrapped his arms around her waist once more, but this time he lifted her shirt and rested his hands on her bare skin. He wanted and needed the connection with her.

Becky could feel his hardness against the small of her back. Jesus. He felt amazing. She shook her head and tried to concentrate as he chuckled, seemingly knowing what she was thinking about.

He leaned down and said right next to her ear, tickling the hair hanging there. "Yes, just a few little yips should do it. As I said before, she knows you're here, it'll be your call to her."

Becky felt utterly ridiculous, and a little off kilter after the amazing kiss she'd shared with Dean, not to mention still feeling his amazing body as he'd cradled her against his body, but she gave it a try anyway.

She howled a bit, softly at first, trying to get the hang of it and to find the right pitch. When she did find a tone that was comfortable and didn't sound too abrasive to her own ears, she increased the volume just a bit and yipped three times.

Dean moved his hand from her waist to her stomach and felt the sounds move through her. He immediately got harder than he already was. Christ. There was no way he could hide it from Becky, seeing how her back was plastered to his front. Her howl broke a bit, but then picked back up again as she yipped some more. He felt her shift and actually push back against him. Holy mother of God…he wasn't going to make it. Sweat broke out on his forehead and the iron control he had on his body almost broke. She might be embarrassed about calling to the coyote, but it was sexy as hell to Dean.

Becky let her voice fade off and waited. She would've waited there forever in Dean's arms, but suddenly she saw a shape off in the distance. It was the little coyote! She was slowly making her way toward them.

Becky gasped and kneeled down, clutching the fence. She was really coming toward them! It'd worked. She looked up at Dean, beaming.

Dean didn't think he'd ever seen anything as beautiful as Becky at that moment.

"She's coming!" Becky said reverently to Dean. He nodded and watched as the little coyote approached them cautiously.

Just as she had earlier, Becky started talking in a low voice. Telling the little coyote that everything was okay, that she had to leave, but she'd hopefully be back. But in the meantime she should trust Dean.

Dean kneeled down next to Becky, reached forward and took her hand in his, holding it close to the fence with his.

Becky understood what he was doing and said, "You can trust him, little star," Becky told the coyote. "He's with me."

Dean could feel Becky hold her breath as the coyote slowly inched her way toward them.

"That's it," she crooned. "You have to trust him and the others, they won't hurt you, they only want to help you."

They stayed like that for a few minutes. Dean and Becky kneeling, with the coyote on the other side, sniffing their interwoven fingers as they gripped the fence. Finally, the coyote rolled over on her back as if to say, 'Rub my belly!'

Becky laughed low.

"I can't rub you today, but I'll be back," she said, hoping she wasn't lying to herself or the coyote. "Go on now, go and find the other coyotes and try to make friends. Be sure to come and get something to eat tomorrow, you're too skinny!"

As if the coyote could understand her, she stood up and ran for the trees. She stopped once, looked back at the two humans and took off again. Becky stood up awkwardly, feeling Dean brace her as she stood.

"Star?" he asked with a smile in his voice.

"She looks like a Star to me," Becky told him sheepishly. "I thought she deserved a beautiful name. She might be small, but she's a Star in my eyes."

Dean hugged Becky to him again, unable to help himself. His woman was so unassuming and unselfish. He was the luckiest man alive.

✵

STEVE INSISTED ON driving Becky back to the production set. Becky sat between him and Dean on the front seat of the truck. She felt very protected between the two large men. She sighed, knowing her lovely night was about to end. She didn't want to go back into the house and deal with the comments and jokes she was sure to get. She also didn't want to continue with the show, but she knew she didn't have a choice. She'd signed the stupid contract and she was obliged. Thank God it was almost over. It couldn't end soon enough for her.

Steve pulled up outside the gates of the house, much

as Dean had the first time he'd dropped her off. Neither man moved. Becky looked from one to the other in confusion, waiting for someone to say something.

Finally, Steve broke the silence.

"Becky, we're thrilled to have met you today and want you to know that we approve of your relationship with Dean. We hope you'll come back soon. We want to get to know you better and we want you to get to know us better."

Becky wasn't sure what to say, so she didn't say anything, but nodded her head in agreement.

Dean took her hand and she turned her attention to him.

"I've told you before, Becky, but I'll tell you again now…you're mine. I'm sorry if that comes out too macho and controlling, I don't mean it to, but when this silly show is over I want you to stay. I want you here with me and my friends and family. I know I'm asking a lot. Believe me, I know it. I get that you have a job and you'd have to move away from your home and friends, but I want to be with you. We can do the long distance thing for a while until you've worked things out back home, but eventually I want you here…with me."

Becky swallowed…hard…opened her mouth to respond, and nothing would come out. She was nervous about the whole situation, but it felt right, and that scared her more than anything else. She didn't think

Dean was being macho and overpowering. At this moment, she wanted to be with him as much as he apparently wanted to be with her. Goosebumps rose on her flesh at the thought of him wanting her as much as he did to brave saying all of these things in front of his dad.

Dean squeezed her hand. "Don't answer now. Think about it for a while, sweetheart, but know, from the bottom of my heart to yours, that I want to be with you. What we have between us is real."

Becky nodded and watched as Dean scooted out of the truck, she followed behind him, turning when Steve spoke.

"Becky, if you ever need anything, please know I'm here for you and so is my wife…anything at all, even if it's just to come out and see your coyote again…we're just a phone call away. Dean will give you our number so you can get in touch with us. Okay?"

Becky nodded her head and finished sliding out of the truck. Dean leaned down and captured her lips with his in a swift, but intense kiss. He then kissed her forehead and held her for a long moment before letting go and stepping back. Becky knew he watched as she let herself through the gate and onto the grounds of the house. The truck didn't pull away until she was safely inside the house. That small act of respect and protection made her smile.

## Chapter Eleven

✦

THE NEXT NIGHT, after another day of the same old crap, Becky lay in bed, waiting for Dean to call. It seemed as if her late night talks with Dean were the only thing keeping her going. There were now only five men left on the show and the pressure was getting to all of them. James, John, Jose, Derek and David were the last contestants. Marissa was unbearable, expecting all five of them to be showering her with attention all the time. She'd even begun playing one against the other, enjoying the jealously they displayed and the lengths they'd go to keep her attention. Marissa hardly talked to Becky anymore, but that was perfectly fine with Becky. Marisa was a raving bitch and Becky didn't want anything to do with her.

The only bright spot in the last week was a visit from Sam and Alex, who were on Eddie's previous reality show in Australia. Eddie had called them and asked if they'd visit the set.

They'd arrived hand in hand and Becky could see

the love they had for each other. It was unexpected, but truly awesome to witness. She didn't think anyone could find love on TV, but they seemed to have done it.

Sam and Alex met with the group that was left and they laughed about Alex's experiences while he was in Australia. Becky noticed that Sam didn't say much, but she seemed to try to be friendly for Alex's sake.

At one point Sam asked if she could talk to Becky alone. Becky jumped at the chance. She really wanted to get Sam's perspective of the whole reality show thing, especially after remembering what Kina had said about how Eddie edited the show. Sam had been where she was. Sam *knew* what she was feeling. At least Becky thought she might.

After settling on a couch on the other side of the room Sam didn't beat around the bush and jumped right into the conversation. "How are you holding up?"

"I'm okay. I'm ready for this whole thing to be over," she answered honestly.

"I bet you are," Sam told her. "Is having two women competing over all the men as bad as it sounds like it'd be?"

"You have no idea!" Becky said with a laugh. "If I had my way, I'd tell Marissa she could have them all and walk off the set today!"

Becky expected Sam to laugh, but was surprised when she not only didn't laugh, but asked, "Why don't you?"

"Uh, because I signed a contract?" Beck said with some surprise. Surely Sam had to sign the same sort of contract when she joined the Australian reality show.

Sam sighed and looked around as if to see if anyone was within earshot. Upon seeing no one, she leaned toward Becky and said softly, "In case you didn't know this, Eddie will do whatever he can to twist the show and make it good for ratings. Even if you *did* walk off at this point, Eddie wouldn't care. He'd probably think it'd be a ratings boon. And in a sick way, he'd be right." Sam laughed with Becky and then continued, "Seriously, Becky, I was on the show for weeks, and he edited me right out of the show just because I didn't fit the mold of what he wanted the women on his show to be. I'm sure he has some twist up his sleeve for this show too. Just be careful."

Becky nodded. Because the conversation had gotten pretty intense, she changed the subject. "So, did you really save Kina's life while you were in Australia?"

Sam laughed and told her the entire story of how Kina was filming her walking around in the Outback and had almost stepped on a deadly snake. She couldn't move or the snake would've bitten her. Sam explained how she'd distracted the snake so Kina could get out of the way.

"Kina wasn't allowed to talk to me on set, for obvious reasons, but after the show was over she contacted me and we've been friends ever since." Sam turned serious again. "She's told me about some of the things that have been happening on this show, Becky." At Becky's blush Sam continued quickly. "Please, don't be embarrassed. I've been in your shoes, literally, and I *know* what you're going through. Keep your chin up. Don't let them get you down. The only reason I agreed to come with Alex to this damn set was to see you. If I had my way I'd never talk to Eddie again. He hurt me. I wasn't pretty enough or good enough to be on his show and he didn't care if I knew it. I don't think I, or Alex, will ever forgive him for that. He certainly knows how to make money, but he doesn't know how to treat people decently."

Sam took Becky's hand in hers and finished, "You're beautiful, Becky. I know you probably can't see it now, but hang in there, finish up the damn show and go on with your life. Things can work out, look at me and Alex!"

Becky squeezed Sam's hand and nodded. She was right. She had to look out for herself and all she had to do was get through the next week of the show and she'd be done with show business for good.

"Thanks for coming today, Sam. It was great to meet you, and I'm so glad you're happy."

The two women hugged each other briefly. Becky

watched as Alex seemed to know exactly when Sam was done talking to her because he came over and grabbed her hand. They laughed together and walked around the set saying hello to the camera operators they'd met while in Australia. Becky watched as both Sam and Alex gave Kina a big hug. Sam hadn't been lying, she and Kina *were* friends. Becky shook off the embarrassment she felt knowing Kina had told the other woman all about what was happening on the set. Oh well, the whole world would know it sooner rather than later, she had to get over it.

Lying in bed, Becky reflected on the day's visit with Sam and Alex. Sam's talk with her helped immensely. It gave her some of her self-esteem back and Becky felt stronger. While she wasn't glad Sam had gone through what she did in Australia, it was nice to know she wasn't alone. Becky was done with the crap the men were giving her and she was done with Marissa. She'd do what she wanted, what she had to do to be done with the show and see if she could work things out with Dean. She knew he wanted to be with her, he'd told her repeatedly, and Becky knew she wanted him back. When she talked to him tonight she'd tell him she'd stay here in Arizona after the show was over. She wanted to give them a chance.

After waiting what seemed to be forever, Becky finally felt the vibration of the disposable phone Dean had given her and eagerly answered it. Expecting to hear Dean, she was surprised to hear a different voice.

"Becky? This is Steve."

Becky sucked in a breath. Why was Steve calling her? It couldn't be good. "Oh my God, is Dean all right?"

Steve was quick to reassure her, "Yes, he's fine. I'm sorry. Jeez, I didn't think. I didn't mean to frighten you."

Becky breathed a sigh of relief. She knew she liked Dean, but she didn't realize how much until she thought Steve was calling to tell her he'd been hurt or worse. She tried to control her adrenaline rush and asked, "What's up?"

"Dean asked me to call. You know he works in security, right?" At Becky's affirmative response he continued, "Well he's going to be out on a job for about four days. He won't be able to contact you as he'll be going up into the mountains around Fresno and won't have any cell service. He wanted to let you know how sorry he was that he couldn't tell you himself. It was a sudden thing and he had to leave right away."

"Is everything all right?" Becky asked.

"It will be," Steve told her. "I can't give you any specific details, but there's a woman who's being stalked and her stalker found where she'd been staying and attacked her. She left town as soon as she could but she's still scared that he'll find her again. Dean was called in to make sure the house she's staying at in the mountains has adequate security and that no one can break in, or if they do get near her, she has time to call for help."

Becky felt bad. Steve sounded almost sad for her.

"It's okay, Steve," she told him brightly. "I'm glad he's going to help that woman. She has to be so frightened. Four days isn't that long and I'll be finishing up this show anyway. If you talk to him, tell him I'm fine and I'll see him when he gets back."

Steve knew Becky wasn't as fine as she was trying to let on, but he also knew if he called her on it, her pride would be hurt.

"Becky, I've told you this before, but if you need anything please don't hesitate to contact me or Jonathan. Even though Dean is out of town, we're still here. Did Dean give you my number? You have it, right?"

"Thanks, Steve, I have it." Becky didn't tell him she wasn't planning on having any need to call him. What could go wrong in four days? Yes, the show was awful, but there wasn't anything that Steve or Jonathan or even Dean could do about it. She'd just have to hang in there, like she'd been doing, until the end of the show and then see if there was anything between her and Dean in the "real world." She was excited about that prospect, just dreading getting through to the end of the show.

Becky thanked Steve again. "Thanks, Steve, I appreciate you calling and letting me know about Dean. I think there's only about a week left on the show and then I'm free!"

"When you're 'free'," Steve said with a laugh, "Let Dean pick you up and bring you here. We'll have a huge party!"

Becky laughed and agreed. They said goodnight to each other and hung up. So much for her relaxing phone call from Dean. She mentally shrugged and snuggled down into the covers to try to catch some sleep so she could make it through the next few days.

## Chapter Twelve

✦

AS THE SHOW was coming to an end, Marissa and the other contestants seemed to get more and more intense, if that was even possible. Becky supposed if she was really interested in any of the men, she'd probably feel the same way. She'd feel pressure at the ceremonies to choose the right guy and if she liked more than one she'd want Marissa to choose the men she liked to stay. But because she didn't care one whit about any of the men, or who Marissa wanted to continue on, it was torture.

Marissa had started coming to her again before the ceremonies to try to tell her who she should choose to stay. She wanted all of her choices to stay, even though she didn't get one hundred percent of the say. In the beginning, Becky would just do what she wanted, but some of the men that were left weren't very nice, at all. In fact, Becky knew if she met any of the men in a bar or anywhere else, they'd probably scare her. Generally they were big, and they were pretty mean. Oh, they were nice to Marissa for sure, but when Marissa wasn't looking they were downright rude, talking about how Becky was an ugly cow and most likely frigid to boot and how they couldn't wait to 'tap' Marissa.

They never did it in front of the cameras, but their comments to Becky as she walked by them were getting worse and worse and downright scary. Derek actually threatened her the other day. They'd been walking past each other in the hallway and he'd stopped her and told her that if she didn't continue to choose him, if Marissa didn't, that she'd regret it.

Becky had tried to talk to Eddie and even the other producers, but they didn't want to hear it. Eddie had practically patted her on the head and said it was all a part of the show. And the other producers wouldn't even take the time to talk to her. Eddie was more concerned that his big investor—Dean—hadn't shown up for the last few days. He'd been told he was away on business, but he didn't believe it and was scrambling to try to figure out what he'd done wrong. Every day he'd grill Jonathan about his "friend" and if he'd be coming back for the show's finale.

Becky didn't dare tell Jonathan or Dean about the threats. She figured she'd just deal with them herself and she'd be sure to never be alone with any of the men who were left on the show. Dean wouldn't be able to do anything, even if he were here for her to talk to. She knew enough about his personality to know it'd be a bad idea to tell him. He was protective of her, as was his dad and even Jonathan, and that made her want to keep this from them. If they did something or said something to any of the men they could get in real trouble. The last thing Becky wanted was to be the cause of trouble for anyone she cared for. Yes, she finally admitted she cared for Dean and his family.

On one of the last days where there were individual dates, Becky had unfortunately "won" a date with Derek. The producers were no longer having Marissa and Becky go on double dates, but letting them go out with the remaining men by themselves. Becky sat in her room before she was supposed to leave on her date with Derek and fingered the phone. Oh, how she wished she could talk to Dean. It'd been a long couple of days and she was kinda scared to go out with Derek. She knew there'd be a camera there, so it wouldn't be like they were truly alone, but she knew Derek didn't like her and she didn't like him in return. It would be very awkward, if nothing else. They had to go out to dinner, and then they were supposed to come back to the house and watch a movie in the TV room.

Becky considered calling Steve for a pre-date pep talk, but then decided that would be ridiculous. She couldn't call her sorta boyfriend's dad before she went on a date with another man. She again reminded herself there was nothing Steve could do and she returned the phone under her pillow. She took a deep breath and walked out of the room. Ready or not, it was time for her date.

Dinner was awkward. Neither of them wanted to be there and they weren't sure what to say to each other. Derek was only interested in winning the stupid show and didn't even try to engage Becky in any meaningful conversation. The only thing he wanted to know about was Marissa and if she was going to choose him to stay at the next ceremony.

After dinner they came back to the house and sat on the couch, on opposite sides, watching a movie. Becky had seen it before and Derek didn't seem remotely interested in what was happening on the screen.

At one point Eddie walked into the room and interrupted them, asking to speak with Derek. They left the room and Derek came back in about five minutes later. He sat very close to Becky and put his arm on the back of the sofa behind her.

Becky was freaking out. What the hell? Derek hadn't shown any affection toward her the entire show, and now, after speaking with Eddie he was suddenly pretending this was a real date? What a joke. Eddie had to have put him up to it.

"What are you doing?" she asked him sharply when he actually had the nerve to put his arm around her shoulder.

"What does it look like, baby?" he asked while winking at the camera that was in the room.

Becky whipped around to see that yes, there was a camera there. The red light blinked at her mockingly, letting her know they were being filmed. She stood up and moved over to the lone chair in the room.

"I don't know you well enough for you to be touching me like that, Derek," she said, knowing she sounded prudish. But seriously? He wanted to pretend to like her now when the entire show he'd been a jerk to her and had actually threatened her the other day? No.

Derek pouted and they both continued to watch the movie. Not long after Eddie left he asked Becky if she was watching the movie. When she shook her head he suggested they call it a night. Becky was all for ending the farce of the date early and settling down, alone, in her bed. She wanted to dream about Dean and hoped that maybe he'd get home early and might call.

Derek offered to walk her to her room. She knew it was just because the cameras were following them. When they got there, she opened her door and when she turned around, Derek was standing right there. He grabbed her in a hug and forced his lips down on hers.

Becky tried to push him away, but he was too strong. He had one hand around the back of her neck, holding her lips to his and the other was like a vice around her waist. He brutally dug his fingers into her side and squeezed. It hurt. Becky tried to break his hold, but he was too strong.

He walked them backwards into her room through the open door. Becky continued to struggle, albeit futilely. Derek's mouth was wet and disgusting, and he was hurting her with the force of both his kiss and his grip on her body.

He finally lifted his head from hers to turn around and grab the door. He blocked Becky's view of the camera, but she heard him say, "I think I'll take it alone from here," in a suggestive tone and he shut the door.

Becky was furious and a little scared. He'd done that on purpose; made it look like they were going to make out in her room, or worse!

When Derek turned back around from the now-closed door she shoved him as hard as she could. Surprisingly, he let go of her, but quickly recovered and shoved her back, hard. Becky went flying and landed hard on her butt on the floor.

Derek came at her again and Becky tried to crab walk backward to keep away from him. She wasn't fast enough and he viciously grabbed her arm and hauled her upright.

Becky was shocked. Although Derek was kind of scary she'd never thought he'd turn violent with her. What the hell was he doing?

She was freaked because she was alone in her room with a man who'd just forced a kiss on her, lied to the camera, held her tight enough to leave bruises, and shoved her across the room. She had to get him out of there.

"Let go of me," Becky said through clenched teeth, trying to wrench her arm out of his grasp.

"No way," Derek hissed. "You owe me," and he threw her around so she landed on her bed.

Becky knew this was quickly getting out of hand. She had no idea what Derek thought she owed him, but she knew she had to do something, fast.

She scrambled across to the other side of the bed before Derek could get a hold of her again. She was *not* going to be raped.

"You asshole," she hissed. "You won't get away with this." Becky looked around the room for her options. She didn't see anything she could use as a weapon. She didn't have her handy baseball bat on the set. She always kept one in her room back home at her apartment. She figured the attached bathroom was her best option at this point.

She knew there was a lock on the door and if she could reach it, then she should be okay, at least theoretically. Of course, Derek could always break the door down, but she didn't *think* he'd go that far. She feigned left and when Derek fell for it and reached for her, she ran to the right and toward the bathroom.

She slammed the door behind her and locked it just as Derek reached the doorknob. He tried it and she could tell he was furious it was locked.

"Open the damn door," he hissed at her, obviously trying to be quiet so everyone else in the house didn't hear him.

Becky didn't answer him, only backed away toward the opposite wall. Like hell she was opening the door. Did he think she was stupid? There was a window in the bathroom, but it was too small for her to climb out of, and besides she was on the second floor. Not to mention she wasn't exactly a ninja and able to land on her feet if she did manage to get out of the stupid thing.

She held her breath, waiting to see what Derek would do. Her heart was beating a million miles an hour and she could feel the adrenaline coursing through her. When Becky heard nothing for ten minutes, she tried to relax. She didn't know if Derek had left or not, he could be trying to wait her out on the other side, but she wasn't leaving this room and the security it offered.

She thought longingly about the phone that was tucked away under her pillow. Damn. She'd give anything to have that phone right now so she could call someone. She knew Dean wasn't around, but Steve *had* said she could call him any time for any reason. This certainly would be a time for her to call him. But there was no way she was leaving the sanctuary of the bathroom. It was amazing what a little wooden door could do to make her feel safe, even if it was only an illusion.

She slid down the wall across from the door to the floor, her knees shaking from the adrenaline rush and reaction to her fright, and put her arms around her knees. She put her head down sideways, resting it on her knees, keeping the door in her sight, just in case. She stayed like that for the rest of the night.

✸

WHEN THE MORNING came Becky almost didn't know what to do. She so badly wanted to talk to Dean, or Jonathan, or even Steve, but what would they be able to do for her now? Nothing. They weren't here. They weren't in charge of this stupid show. She was stuck, complaining to them wouldn't solve anything, and certainly telling Eddie wouldn't work. She tried to shake some sense into herself. She was an adult woman who could handle this on her own. She didn't need any help.

She thought back to the night before how it wasn't until after Eddie had talked to Derek that he'd come up with the idea to walk her to her room. It was obvious Eddie had given the suggestion to Derek. If Becky had been raped it would've been as much Eddie's fault as it was Derek's. She truly felt that way.

Becky felt sick. She was outnumbered and had no

allies on this show. None. She was done. She had a black and blue mark on her arm where Derek had grabbed her, her tailbone was sore after landing on it where he'd shoved her. She also had bruising around her waist from where Derek had held her to him as he pushed them through her bedroom door in front of the camera. Becky knew she'd been lucky and it was time to end this farce. Dean wasn't home from wherever he was, but she couldn't wait any longer.

She cautiously opened the bathroom door and peeked out. The bedroom was empty. Nothing seemed out of place, but Becky wasn't taking any chances. The first thing she checked was the phone, it was still there. She grabbed it and the rest of her things and put them in her suitcase. She went back into the bathroom with her bag and locked the door and took a quick shower. She had to be ready. She'd be leaving the show today, and she knew just how she'd do it. She had to do it while the cameras were rolling so no one could say or do anything. If she did it in "public," then she'd be all right, she reasoned with herself. Once she got off this show she could start her life again. Hopefully with Dean.

## Chapter Thirteen

✦

Later that afternoon was another ceremony. The five men who were left stood in their spots. Both Becky and Marissa were supposed to choose two to stay. Marissa, of course, came to her before the ceremony and informed her of who she was supposed to vote to keep.

Becky didn't say anything. She just let Marissa think she was going along with what she wanted. Whatever. Becky was so done with Marissa and the stupid show. She actually couldn't believe Marissa still had the nerve to try to tell her who she should choose to keep. After everything that had happened so far and everything that had been said between the two of them, it was completely ridiculous.

Finally, it was time. Robert had a dramatic speech about how the end was nearing and how everyone was on pins and needles to see who'd be staying this time and who'd be going home.

When Robert finally finished with his soliloquy, it

was once again Marissa's turn to make her choices. She stood up in front of the men and the cameras and gave a long speech about how hard the decision was and how it was the hardest decision yet, which every reality show contestant in the history of reality television always said, and the same thing that Marissa said every damn week. She chose to keep Jose and John.

Then it was Becky's turn. There were three men left, one of which was Derek. Becky knew which two Marissa wanted her to keep. She'd gone on and on to her about how cute Derek and David were and what great TV it made that they were also twins. It'd be such a great theatrical ending if the two of them ended up as the final choices.

Everyone was staring at Becky intently. The cameras were caching the drama on film. Eddie was watching to make sure his money-train kept clacking along. Derek, David, and James were watching her, staring at her, hoping to somehow influence her telepathically to choose them so they'd have another chance at winning Marissa and becoming famous in the process. Robert and Marissa were looking at her expectantly, waiting for her to start.

Becky took a deep breath.

"This week the decision is an easy one for me," Becky said clearly, being sure to look at each camera in the room before turning back to the men. She wasn't going to make a long speech and blame people for the miserable experience. She just wanted it done.

"I choose…" She paused, dragging out the moment for dramatic effect. "No one."

No one said anything at first and it was so quiet Becky could hear the grandfather clock in the corner ticking. Had they heard her? Surely they had.

When Marissa finally gasped, Becky continued, "I don't feel compatible with any of the men that are left, and I'm sure they don't feel compatible with me. The last dates I've been on haven't gone well, and it's obvious the men who are remaining would rather be with Marissa than with me. I'm okay with that. It was never guaranteed I'd find the man of my dreams on the show."

Becky thought she was laying it on a big thick, but she continued anyway, "After last night," she couldn't help herself and glared at Derek, "it was brought home even more to me that I need to move on. I'm forfeiting my choice tonight and would like for Marissa to finish the show. She can choose two more men of her liking, or less, depending on how the producers would like to proceed. I wish her, and all of you," she nodded to the remaining men, "the best of luck."

Eddie called out, "Cut!" and stormed onto the set.

"You can't do that!" he raged at Becky. She didn't even flinch.

"I just did," she told him defiantly, wondering where her backbone had been up until now. "You set me up to be the pathetic second-choice woman from the start. Well, I'm done. I played your game long enough. It's obvious none of the men are going to choose me," she said, waving her hand in the direction of the remaining contestants. "And I think you knew that would happen from the start. You'd better just take what I've done and run with it. It's a great twist to the show and you can continue on as planned with just Marissa and the remaining men. I'm done."

Becky looked Eddie straight in the eyes as she spoke. He knew she was dead serious and for the first time in a long time was flustered and out of his element. He hadn't seen this coming. Usually *he* was the one driving the twists and turns in his shows.

"You won't get a dime, this is a breach of contract," he sputtered at her meanly, not knowing what else to do.

"I don't care," Becky retorted, "I just want out of this house and off this show."

She turned around and walked toward the door. She passed Jonathan on her way and he reached out to take her by the arm. Becky flinched, he'd managed to grab the same spot that Derek had last night and it was still painful.

Jonathan saw her flinch and his eyes narrowed.

"What the hell? Are you all right? What's really going on?" he asked urgently.

Becky laughed awkwardly. "Of course, Jonathan, I just humiliated myself for the last time on National TV, why wouldn't I be okay?" She willed the tears not to fall. She had to make it through this last bit before she fell apart.

Jonathan didn't like the look in Becky's eyes, and he certainly didn't like the way she'd flinched from his touch. He knew he hadn't grabbed her that roughly. What was going on? Dean should be here, Becky needed him.

"Dammit!" He swore softly. He knew he couldn't get off the set until the shoot was over. And after Becky's bombshell he knew they wouldn't be leaving anytime soon. Eddie would have to regroup and figure out how to best use Becky's actions to make the show a success. His hands were tied. He'd call his dad as soon as he could. Maybe he could go and see Becky or could somehow get a hold of Dean. His brother was going to be pissed he wasn't there for Becky when everything had gone down.

The cameras followed Becky as she left the house, suitcase in hand and got into the limo. Kina happened to be the camera operator on duty and sat across from Becky in the limo and filmed her as they pulled away from the house. Becky knew they were going to a local hotel. She refused to look at the camera, just stared out the window at the passing scenery. She had to stay there until the end of the show, just as all of the other men on the show who'd been dismissed had to. She hoped she wouldn't run into any of them, it could get complicated. She didn't know if they'd be mad at her or if they would even care.

Kina put down the camera and looked at Becky.

"That was the best thing I've seen on this show so far," she told Becky with a smile. "In fact, I think it was the best thing I've seen in *any* of the shows I've filmed."

Becky smiled weakly back at her, but didn't really have anything witty to say back to her. She was done. Mentally just done.

"They're all assholes, Becky, you just keep being you, you're okay."

Becky just stared at her. Okay, well, at least everyone on the show didn't see her as pathetic.

"We all think that way, you know," she reminded her. "All the camera operators, that is. We've seen all of the crap they've put you through and you've definitely come through it looking like the better person. We'll be sorry to see you go, Becky, you've been the only interesting part of this show!"

Kina leaned forward, touched her knee and looked Becky in the eye. "Seriously, Becky. Men are assholes. I've never met one I'd trust with my life. I thought I had once, but I was wrong. Way wrong. Don't be like me. My heart is frozen to the core. I'm a hard woman and don't ever see any man being able to thaw me out. But you…" She paused, and seemed to fight back some sort of emotion, then continued, "You're a good person. Please don't let this experience, and these jerks change you. There's a guy out there for you, you just have to keep looking."

Becky pondered what Kina said and nodded. "I know, I think I've already found him," she told Kina honestly.

Kina smiled at her as they arrived at the hotel. She helped her out of the seat and waved as she turned to go into the hotel. As Becky got to the door of the hotel she looked back and watched as the limo headed back to the production house. Becky was sad for Kina. She didn't know her story, but it had to have been something awful for her to believe she'd never find anyone for herself.

Becky couldn't wait to get to her room, take a shower and process all that had happened. She wanted to talk to Dean, but she didn't really know what to say yet. Besides, she had no idea if he was even back from the job he was on. She decided she'd call him later. There was no need to call Steve either. She was out of the house and off the show. It wasn't as if she was allowed out of the hotel. She had to stay until the end of the show.

It was as if a huge weight had been lifted off of her shoulders. She could be herself again. She didn't have to worry about cameras being around, or about watching what she said and what she did for fear it'd be taped and end up on television. Becky was ready to relax for a few days and then get back to her life. A life that hopefully would include Dean and his incredible family.

## Chapter Fourteen

✦

AFTER A LONG, hot shower and a short nap, Becky felt a hundred percent better. It was amazing the amount of stress she felt lifted from her shoulders as a result of not being on the show or around the set anymore. She wasn't sure how long she'd have to stay in the hotel, but she figured someone would let her know the show was over. They were, after all, paying the bill. She should be thankful of that, considering how pissed Eddie was at her.

Becky decided to make her way downstairs to the restaurant. She was starving. She was looking forward to a nice big salad and a bowl of soup. She was seated in the restaurant near the front window. It was interesting to watch the comings and goings of the other guests from the lobby. Lord knew she didn't have anything else to entertain her. She ordered her food and it didn't take long for it to arrive.

Eating and not having to carry on a conversation at the same time was awesome. It was just as great to not have to worry about a camera catching her with food in her teeth or dribbling down her chin. It was awkward to eat and know you were being filmed.

Just as she was finishing up her soup she noticed a limo pull up in front of the hotel's lobby. She watched as two men got out. Holy crap! It was the twins, Derek and David! She about choked on her soup. This wasn't happening! She thought she'd gotten away from Derek by leaving the show, but somehow it looked like Marissa didn't choose to keep him *or* his brother on the show. Becky wondered how that came about. Marissa had been adamant that both men be allowed to stay. After all, she'd said, you couldn't split up a pair of twins. Becky knew she'd have to avoid them at all costs. It was better if they didn't know she was here.

That would be easier said than done. As per the contract rules, contestants weren't allowed to be seen "out and about," so they were essentially kept prisoner in the hotel. They were allowed to freely roam the grounds, but they weren't supposed to leave. In some ways it was worse than being on the actual show. She couldn't image what the men like Ned and Oliver had gone through. They left the show in the first ceremony and had been at the hotel a long time.

Later that night, Becky finally tried to call Dean. He didn't answer, which wasn't totally surprising as his dad had said he probably wouldn't have any cell service where he was going, so she left him a message. She didn't mean to be cryptic, but it was just too complicated to try to explain everything that had happened over the phone.

*Hey Dean,* she said softly after the beep sounded, letting her know she could leave a message. *I miss you. I hope everything is going okay with your job. Your dad told me a bit about what you're doing, I hope that's all right. I know you'll make that woman feel safe. I know I always feel safe when I'm around you. I know you won't let anything happen to me. Anyway, some stuff happened on the show today, nothing bad, but it's kinda complicated and too long to tell you in a message. I'll talk to you soon and tell you all about it. Be safe. Don't worry about me and hopefully I'll see you soon. I wanted to tell you as well, that…well…if you still want me to, I want to stay here and get to know you better…okay, well, call me when you get back. Bye.*

After sitting around her hotel room for a few hours, Becky was bored. The thought of sitting in her room watching any more boring television wasn't appealing. Even though she hadn't seen any television the entire time she'd been in the production house, it just wasn't cutting it. She supposed she'd been weaned off it.

She'd eaten a late lunch and, while she wasn't hungry enough for a full dinner, Becky figured she could get an appetizer and that would tide her over. She could've ordered room service, but she was already going stir crazy. She decided she'd just go downstairs and grab something quick and get back up here to her room.

As she made her way into the restaurant she saw Derek, his twin, and some of the other men from the show in the bar area. They'd obviously been there a while as they were loud and quite drunk.

Becky shrugged her shoulders and went into the restaurant. She'd just stay away from the bar. Soon after she ordered, Derek and his twin suddenly appeared at her table.

"Can we join you?" Derek asked snidely, pulling out the chair and sitting without giving her a chance to answer him.

Becky's heart rate doubled. Crap. This was not good. This was not good. This was not good. She hadn't talked to Derek after he'd tried to rape her and she hadn't seen him other than at the last ceremony. David also sat down and didn't say a word. That was almost creepier than if he'd said hello or even if he'd said something rude.

Derek leaned close to her and growled, "You bitch, you ruined my chance to be famous and my chance with Marissa. You also ruined his chances too," pointing toward his brother.

"But I didn't make you leave." Becky tried to explain, shrinking back into the squeaky pleather of the booth. She looked around, hoping to see someone, anyone, that might notice what was going on and help her. Of course, no one was around.

"Yeah, well, after you left, Eddie changed the game and would only allow Marissa to keep one more guy. She decided if she couldn't have both of us, she didn't want either of us. So because you decided to quit, we had to leave. It's directly your fault, cunt. You have to pay for that!"

Becky's heart almost stopped. She had no idea Eddie would do anything so drastic. She figured Marissa would be able to choose two men to stay in her place. No wonder Derek was so pissed. It was also pure Marissa to decide to ditch both Derek and David. What good was one twin to her? It wouldn't pull in nearly enough attention. Becky swallowed hard and tried to think of something to say to get herself out of the situation.

Derek dragged her out of the booth by her arm, squeezing in the same place he'd gripped her the day before. Becky opened her mouth to protest, to scream, something…after all she was in a public place.

Derek gripped her arm even harder, digging his fingernails into her skin cruelly and said, "If you say anything, you'll only make it worse for yourself. You want to make a scene? Go ahead, we'll claim that you're bipolar and having an episode. Who do you think they'll believe? You? An ugly fat hag? Or us? Gorgeous, muscular twins who are only concerned about their poor crazy sister?"

Becky shut up. She was scared to death. What were they planning? Maybe she could talk them down when they got out of the restaurant. David still hadn't said a word, but obviously was supportive of anything his brother did. He threw a twenty dollar bill on the table to cover her meal and the three of them walked out of the restaurant and to the elevators.

Becky noticed they were going to the eighth floor. Hers was on the fourth floor.

She swallowed hard and finally said, "What the hell are you doing, Derek? Let me go, seriously, get over it." She pretended to have more bravado than she actually had. "This is ridiculous, what will this do? Get you back on the show? No, it's only going to make things worse!" She tried to reason with him as well as David. "David, seriously, I had nothing to do with you getting kicked off the show. You can't be serious." When both Derek and David ignored her, she resorted to pleading with them.

"Please, guys, don't do this. Let me go. I'll go back to the set and say whatever you want. I'll tell Eddie I want back on the show and you can come back and I'll choose you both. I swear it. Please…" Her voice fell off as they dragged her down the hall to room eight twelve. Where the hell were all the guests? Why wasn't anyone around?

Derek opened the door and pushed her in the room with David following close on their heels. Becky knew once they got her in their room she was screwed. She watched as the hotel door closed behind them. David turned to the door and locked it while Derek dragged her to the bed.

✵

BECKY WOKE UP the next morning slowly. She tried to roll over and gasped. She hurt everywhere. She looked around. She was alone in the room. She thought frantically…where were Derek and David? Did they leave her alone momentarily with plans to come back and continue where they left off? Becky painfully pulled herself to a sitting position. She was naked. She could see her clothes strewn about the room. She shakily stood up and forced herself to gather up her clothes. She wanted out of this room now. Finally, mostly dressed, she made her way to the stairwell. She didn't want to chance using the elevators in case the twins were making their way back to the room. She walked down the four flights to her floor and cautiously opened the door. The hallway was empty, thank God. She went to her room and slipped in, miraculously her room key was still in the pocket of her pants. She walked numbly to the bathroom and stared at herself in the mirror.

Even she was shocked. Her face looked like she'd gone three rounds with a boxer. She had two black eyes and her face was swollen to twice its normal size. She opened her mouth and saw that her front tooth had a chip in it. She didn't remember when that happened, but she supposed it had been when Derek had hit her…one of the times.

She sat on the toilet seat and tried to get her breath. Her chest hurt, probably because she'd been held down. David had sat on her chest at one point because she wouldn't stay still. Her arms were covered in bruises from being held as well. She'd fought them until she'd finally passed out.

She stifled a hysterical laugh at the black permanent marker all over her body. Apparently the twins had a problem with alcohol and being able to get it up. They'd tried to rape her, but the fact she wouldn't quit fighting them combined with the alcohol in their system wouldn't allow them to be able to hold an erection.

When they couldn't get their dicks to cooperate they'd gotten out the permanent marker. For some reason they thought it would be hilarious to write all over her. The words were obscene in their starkness. Whore. Bitch. Cunt. Fat. Cow. Stupid. They'd tried to get creative and couldn't really think of too many other derogatory words in their inebriated state. Most of the words were smeared. Some were illegible because again,

Becky wouldn't lie still and let them have their fun.

They'd also spit on her. Over and over. Calling her names and saying she wasn't worth the ground she walked on. At one point she thought she remembered them having a contest to see who could hawk the biggest loogie and hit her in the face with it. She shuddered with revulsion.

She sobbed once and then ruthlessly choked it back. If she started crying, she didn't know if she'd be able to stop. She continued to take stock of her body. The writing on her skin wasn't physically painful, only mentally so. She was sore from being held down and fighting them. She could walk, so her legs weren't broken, but she thought she might have a broken collarbone. It hurt like hell. She'd once broken her collarbone when she was little. A cast wouldn't work. All they did was put her arm in a sling and told her to be careful.

Becky thought about what she should do next. If she took a shower she'd probably wash away any physical evidence Derek and David left on her, but would anything happen if she went to the police? She'd probably have to testify, and the last thing she wanted to do was see the twins again.

The hell with it. She slowly got up and stripped off her clothes. She was in a state of shock, she knew it, but she couldn't deal with anything right now other than taking a shower to get clean and getting the hell out of there.

The shower was longer than she'd planned, but she just couldn't get clean. She scrubbed at her face to get the feeling of their spit off of her. It hurt, bad, but she didn't stop. The marker wouldn't come off her skin no matter how hard she scrubbed. She used the washcloth and rubbed her skin until it was red and raw and she could still see the words. Cow. Bitch. Cunt.

She couldn't stop remembering the laughs and the taunts and the pain as the men took turns holding her down and writing on her. As they swore at her as they tried to get it up. They hit her when they couldn't and blamed her for being butt ugly and a cow.

Their words haunted her.

Finally, she made herself get out of the shower. Becky knew she'd ruined her best chances of the men paying for what they did, but it was hard to think. She did take the trash can liner out of the can and put the clothes she'd been wearing in it. She figured it might be better than nothing if she decided down the line to press charges, but that was as far as she could go in trying to preserve any evidence.

She got dressed again, jeans and a long sleeved shirt to cover her arms, and a sweatshirt. She couldn't get warm. She knew it was shock, but she didn't stop to think about it. She packed up the rest of her belongings and left the room. She didn't even tell the front desk she was leaving. The hell with the show, the hell with Eddie, and the hell with the hotel.

She went out a side door and walked to the nearest fast food restaurant. She asked the manager to call a cab, and as a testimony to what her face looked like, he didn't even question her other than asking if she was all right.

Ten minutes later she was in the cab. When the driver asked her where she wanted to go, Becky's mind immediately flashed to Dean and his family. She shook her head. She couldn't go there in her mind yet. But she did want to say goodbye to Star. Something pulled her toward the little coyote and Becky wanted to make sure she was okay before she left. She gave the driver directions, put her head back on the seat and closed her eyes.

✶

JONATHAN TRIED TO call his brother a few times after his shift on the show was over, but he wasn't answering his phone. It wasn't necessarily unusual because he knew Dean was up in the mountains and most of the time there wasn't cell service up there. But Jonathan was worried about Becky. After she left in the limo, Eddie decided that Marissa had to choose two men to leave rather than only one more, as it would've been originally.

Marissa pitched a fit. Jonathan heard her yelling at Eddie behind a closed door. She was stomping her feet and wanting to change her original choices as a result of Becky leaving. Eddie refused to let her.

Jonathan knew Marissa was heartless, but he hadn't realized she didn't have a speck of honor in her body when he heard her tell Eddie without a speck of remorse, "Fine, David and Derek will have to go then because it's no good to only have one twin. They're only good if they're together."

He knew the contestants who were no longer on the show were brought to a hotel to wait out the show. Jonathan stopped by last night after filming to see if he could get a hold of Becky, but there was no answer when he was transferred to her room by the hotel operator.

They, of course, wouldn't give him her room number so he had no way of getting a hold of her and thus no choice but to leave. His instincts were telling him something wasn't right, but he had nothing to go on and he couldn't get a hold of Becky. He decided he'd keep trying to call Dean and would get a hold of Becky the next day. If he had to he'd get his dad involved and see if he could get a hold of Dean, somehow.

✹

BECKY OPENED HER eyes when the cab stopped near the

front gates of the refuge.

"Ya want me to pull in, lady?" the driver asked gruffly. He'd seen how badly she'd been beaten and felt sorry for her. He'd wanted to bring her to the hospital, but Becky refused. She wasn't ready.

She quickly answered, "No, please, just pull over here…and…if it's not too much to ask…can you wait for me? I promise I won't be long…I just…there's something I have to do."

The driver turned around and looked at the pathetic woman in his cab.

"You're not going to do something illegal, are you?" he asked sternly. "Or hurt yourself?"

"Oh, no!" Becky answered quickly. "I just have to say goodbye to someone before I leave town."

The driver gazed at the woman for several moments and once again tried to urge her to let him take her to a doctor. When she refused he finally gave in and said, "Okay, but the meter's runnin'." Becky nodded. Thank God cabs took credit cards nowadays.

She stepped out of the cab and walked a little ways down the fence line along the gravel road. She went around a small corner and sat on the ground gingerly. It hurt too much to crouch.

She very softly howled and yipped just as Dean had taught her what seemed so long ago. She really wanted to see Star. She wasn't sure why, but she just wanted to be sure she was all right and had been eating.

After a minute or so she heard movement in the trees surrounding the fence. Suddenly the coyote was there. She walked straight up to the fence with no hesitation and whined. Becky stuck her fingers through the fence. Again, maybe not the smartest thing she'd ever done, but hell, nothing could make her feel worse right now. What was a dog bite added to everything else?

"Hey, girl…you okay? I wanted to come and see you again…before I left…"

Becky felt a tear fall down her face. She sniffed. "I'm gonna miss you, girl. Have you been eating? And making friends?"

The coyote stared at Becky and tilted her head. It was as if the coyote could really see her, could really understand her. She whined again and licked Becky's fingers through the fence.

Becky's tears fell harder. "Oh God, Star…" Becky's voice trailed off. The coyote had gotten a hold of the sleeve of Becky's sweatshirt and was pulling on it…as if to say, "follow me."

Becky pulled back on the material, and heard it tear. Ignoring her torn clothing, she looked over toward the bend in the road where she hoped the cab was still waiting on her. She knew another car could come by and catch her…and she didn't want anyone in Dean's family to see her looking like she was. She wished she was braver and could go to Steve and Bethany and ask for help. But she was embarrassed and humiliated and didn't want anyone to see her, especially the awful words that she couldn't scrub off her body.

"I have to go, Star," Becky said, finally tugging her sleeve free. "I wish I could stay. I wish I could be a part of this family, but I can't…" The coyote whined. "You just don't understand, Star…I can't go to him…he can't see me…" Her voice trailed off. Through her tears she managed to say, "You be a good girl. I'll miss you." She slowly stood up, wiped the tears from her face and made her way back to the cab.

✸

THE SAME AFTERNOON Becky said goodbye to the little coyote, Dean arrived back into town and went straight to the refuge. The security job hadn't been tough physically, but it'd been torture for Dean mentally. He'd seen what the stalker had done to the woman and he'd made it his mission to make her feel as safe as possible. He'd patiently gone over and over the codes to the alarms and explained how they worked, just so she'd feel okay about her safety after he left.

Satisfied he'd done all he could, Dean made his way back home and to his *One*. He'd missed her terribly and felt bad he hadn't been able to talk to her while he was gone. He never liked being out of touch with his family for long periods of time, but there was no way he was going to leave the woman alone up in the mountains until he'd set up all the security systems.

He'd listened to Becky's phone message earlier and at first couldn't think about anything else but about how she'd told him she wanted to give them a chance and wanted to stay here with him. His heart leapt with joy. It wasn't until he couldn't get a hold of her when he'd called her back that he'd started to get concerned. He wondered if whatever happened on the show had something to do with it. He didn't like not having all the details and he definitely didn't like not being able to reach her. It made him twitchy, especially coming off of the job he had.

Now, heading to the refuge he still hadn't been able to connect with Becky. It was making him more than a little uneasy. He wanted to be able to see her and hold her to be sure everything was all right. He'd gotten used to being able to talk to her every day. He wanted to hear about what happened on the show and to make sure she was all right. He knew Becky had been having issues and desperately wanted to leave the set, and it killed him that he couldn't help her. All he could do was listen and try to support her from afar.

Dean pulled up to the house at the refuge center to talk to his dad and decompress. Helping with the animals was the best therapy he'd ever found, even if helping was mucking out the barn, and he was glad to be home. He cut the engine on his truck and massaged the kinks out of his neck. He'd been traveling a long time and wanted nothing more than to see and talk to Becky and possibly go for a run, in that order. He headed toward the house. The sooner he talked to his dad the sooner he'd hopefully see his woman.

The house was in chaos when he opened the door. The hair stood up on the back of his neck. All thoughts of being tired disappeared and he quickly walked over to his father. Steve saw him when he walked in the door and went over to intercept him.

"What's going on?" Dean asked quickly as he approached.

"Becky's missing." Steve told him without beating around the bush.

"What?" Dean roared, feeling dizzy. How could she be missing? What did he mean?

Steve steered his son toward a chair and motioned for the other employees to clear the room. Dean finally noticed Jonathan standing near their mother.

"What happened?" Dean asked again firmly.

Jonathan answered, "We don't know, bro'. She took herself off the show and then she disappeared."

Dean's head spun. Was this what she'd wanted to tell him that night?

"Start from the beginning," Dean ordered tightly.

Jonathan recounted the events from the other night. How Becky had enough of the show and essentially voted herself off. He explained what went down after she left with the twins and Marissa and how he went to the hotel after he was released from the set and couldn't get a hold of her. He explained how the next day, when he finally convinced a hotel employee to check on her, her room was empty. She'd left. They'd tried to track her down, with no luck. No one had seen her leave and they didn't know where she'd gone.

✹

DEAN SAT IN front of his brother and parents and tried to think about what to do next. He worked in security for a living, he should know what to do, but he couldn't wrap his mind around the fact that his *One* had just left…it felt like she'd left *him*. Had she not wanted to be with him after all? She said on the phone message she wanted to stay, had she changed her mind?

He thought he'd made it clear he wanted to be with her, that she was his. Had Dean come on too strong? Had Becky decided he was too protective, too controlling? Too many questions were chasing through his head at once. He shook his head as if to clear it…and realized the noise he heard wasn't coming from inside him, but from outside in the pen, it was a coyote…howling mournfully out in the yard. Howling like that was unusual for a coyote. They were much more likely to communicate by yipping. He looked out the window, then back at his dad.

"She's been doing that for a while now. We can't get her to come near us, and she won't stop howling," Steve said.

Chills ran down Dean's back. It was Star. He knew it. She knew something, she was trying to communicate with them, but he hadn't been home. He knew how hard it was for the little coyote to trust. People generally didn't give animals enough credit. They knew when something was wrong. There were so many stories of dogs predicting earthquakes and other bad weather. Had Becky come back to see "her" coyote before she'd left? She had to have. How else would the coyote know to be upset?

He stood up so fast the chair he'd been sitting in was knocked to the ground. He strode toward the door, Steve and Jonathan following close behind. He went toward the gate and let himself into the enclosure. He walked toward the sound. Steve and Jonathan stayed back at the fence to watch. They'd both tried to get close to the little coyote with no luck. Every time they'd tried, the coyote had run off into the bush, only to return and start howling again once they'd left. Perhaps Dean could get near her. It was worth a shot.

Dean knew it wasn't like he'd be able to talk to the animal, but maybe he could at least calm her down. It was breaking everyone's hearts to hear the little coyote howl so mournfully.

Dean strode through the enclosure toward the tree line. He followed the sound of the coyote's howling. He slowed down when he saw the little coyote. She was sitting staring at the fence that lined the road to their refuge. Becky had to have been here. Why else would the coyote be sitting right there?

He said softly, "Star, what is it? What's wrong? Do you know what happened to my *One*? Where is she?"

He didn't know what to expect. He didn't think the coyote would suddenly stand up and start talking, but he sure didn't expect her to come running toward him and leap at him. He automatically caught her as he fell backward. Dean hoped she wasn't attacking him. He'd hate to harm her, but he'd protect himself.

As he lay on his back the coyote just stood over him. Staring at him. Staring into his eyes. Dean repeated more urgently, not even thinking about how silly it was to be talking to an animal as if it would answer him. "You know what happened, don't you? Oh God, I wish you could talk, where is she?"

Star backed off of Dean and kept backing up until she was a distance away from him. She howled again. Another mournful howl. Dean sat up and watched the coyote as she turned toward the fence once more and trotted over to it. She picked something up from the ground with her teeth and brought it over to where Dean was still sitting on the ground.

It was a piece of fabric. A small one, but it proved to Dean that Becky had more than likely been there. This coyote was smart. Dean looked at her again, closely. It dawned on him for the first time that she was probably mixed with some sort of dog. Many times coyotes would mate with feral dogs or even neighborhood dogs that were out and running around. Maybe that was why she was more willing to play with Becky and why she had such a close bond with her.

He stood up slowly, the material clutched tightly in his hand. Something was terribly wrong. He knew it. Becky wouldn't have come to say goodbye to the little coyote if she was coming back. Something had happened. Dean's stomach got tight, if she'd been hurt…enough of this bullshit. He had to do something. Becky wasn't leaving him without a word. He'd find her and fix whatever had happened to spook her.

Dean turned and started back toward the house. Surprisingly the coyote followed him closely, as if she knew he'd take care of her new friend.

When Dean arrived at the gate to the pen, he turned around and kneeled to face the little coyote. He held out his hand and she came to him without hesitation. Dean scratched her ears and bent toward her, saying for her ears only, "Thank you, Star. I'll get her back, I promise."

He then stood up and left the enclosure, heading back to where his family was standing. He saw that his brother was talking on the phone and listening intently to whomever was on the other side. Finally, he hung up.

"I had a hunch and called around to a few taxi companies. If she did leave the hotel she had to have gotten a ride from someone. She doesn't have a car here, so I figured she'd take a taxi somewhere."

The others nodded and Dean impatiently gestured for him to continue. He wasn't usually so brusque, but this was his woman and he was beyond worried about her.

Jonathan continued, "I got lucky and the second company I called had a record of picking up a woman from a restaurant near the hotel around the general time I figured she'd left. I got even luckier and got to talk to the driver himself." He paused and looked at his brother. "You're not going to like what he said, Dean."

Dean nodded. "I don't like any of this. Go on."

"He said she looked like she'd been beaten up," Jonathan said bluntly, knowing now wasn't the time to sugarcoat anything. They had to get to the bottom of what happened to Becky and find her. "She did come to the refuge. The driver said she asked to come here and he stopped outside the gates. She asked for him to wait and she went around the corner where he couldn't see her and was gone about ten minutes. When she came back she was crying. He tried again to get her to let him take her to a doctor, but she refused."

"Where did he finally drop her off?" Dean asked impatiently, trying to come to terms with all he'd learned in the last few minutes.

"He brought her to another hotel on the other side of the city," Jonathan said.

"Why didn't she come to us?" Bethany asked.

No one said anything for a moment until Dean finally answered the question he figured everyone was thinking. "I think she was embarrassed. She didn't want to be a burden. I've talked to her on the phone almost every night she's been in that house and on the show and gotten to know her pretty well. She wanted to let her little coyote know she didn't abandon her, but whatever happened must have humiliated and embarrassed her and she wasn't ready to see anyone."

"But Dean," his mom said haltingly. "She's your *One*, doesn't she know you'd protect her and she'd never have any reason to be embarrassed with you?"

"For starters," Dean tried to explain something he wasn't sure he completely understood. "She doesn't really know you guys. She only knows you're my family. Sure, she knows me pretty well after all our conversations, but remember, I wasn't here. She'd have to deal with you guys. She had no idea when I'd be back." His voice broke on the last word. He hadn't been here for her. On one hand he knew it wasn't his fault. He was working, it wasn't like he was away on a pleasure cruise, but on the other hand, irrationally, it felt like he'd let down the most important person in his life.

Dean cleared his throat and tried to ignore the compassionate looks his family was giving him. They knew how much this was hurting him. "The first instinct anyone has, be that a person or an animal, when they're hurt is to hide. We want to get away from what's scaring or hurting us. I've seen it over and over again with the women I help set up personal security for. I'm hoping I can find Becky and let her know that this is *her* refuge as much as it is an animal's. She can always come here to hide if I can't be around to let her hide in my arms."

He looked at his family standing around him, supporting him. "I'll find her," he said resolutely. "Jonathan, give me the address of the hotel she was dropped off at. I'll start there."

"I'll go with you," Jonathan said without hesitation.

God, Dean loved his family. They'd do anything for him without asking for anything in return. That loyalty was one reason why he still lived near his folks. He was so grateful Jonathan was making his way back to Arizona as well. He loved having him back in his life.

Steve's phone rang shrilly, startling everyone. He pulled it out of his pocket and saw it was an unknown number.

"Hello?"

"Hi. Uh, Steve?"

Steve frantically motioned to Dean as he answered. "Yes, Becky, it's me. Where are you? Are you okay? We've been worried sick about you." There was so much more he wanted to say, but first things first. They had to find her. Dean had to find her.

Becky answered softly, "I'm going to be fine. I'm so sorry I didn't call you right away. I know you said I could, I just…" Her voice faded off.

Dean was reaching for the phone at the same time Steve was holding it out toward him. Steve knew Dean had to talk to her.

"Sweetheart?" he said softly but urgently. "Tell me where you are and I'll come and get you. Whatever happened we'll get through together, okay?"

He heard her sniff and it about killed him.

Becky had to get the tough apology out of the way first. She knew with Dean's sense of family loyalty she was going to have to answer to that first of all. She repeated what she'd said to his dad. "I'm sorry I didn't call your dad or brother before."

"You're calling now, sweetheart, it's all that matters. Where are you?" Dean asked again. He didn't want to break the connection until he found that out.

He heard her take a deep breath. "I'm in town, I'm at the hospital." At his sharp inhalation she continued on quickly, "But I'm all right, Dean, I promise."

"We're on our way," he said to her, already walking toward his truck. His family immediately mobilized as well. There was no way they were letting Dean go without them. They figured both he and Becky would need their unwavering support to get through whatever happened.

"No, wait, don't hang up," Becky pleaded frantically, not wanting him to hang up. Now that she'd made the decision to call and now that she was actually talking to Dean, she didn't want to let him go.

"I'm not going anywhere, sweetheart," Dean said soothingly. "I'm not hanging up."

Becky sniffed again, frantically trying to hold her tears back. God, she couldn't lose it now. "I know you want to know what happened," she started hesitantly.

"Actually, no," Dean said surprisingly. "I want to wait for you to tell me where you've been and what happened while I have you safe in my arms."

There was dead silence on the other end of the line for a moment, then Dean heard her sobbing.

"Oh, Becky, God, please don't. Please don't cry when I'm not there with you. Hang on, I'll be there as soon as I can."

Becky tried to get it together. God, he never stopped surprising her with the sweet things he said. She figured most people would be clamoring to get the entire story immediately. She didn't want to tell him about the whole humiliating experience, but she didn't have a choice. One part of her wanted to tell him on the phone so she wouldn't have to face him, but that obviously wasn't going to happen. She had to warn him, though.

"Uh, Dean," she said, knowing he wasn't going to like what she said next.

"Yes, sweetheart?"

Becky could hear the truck start up and hear Jonathan in the background talking to someone. It looked like Dean's entire family was on their way as well. Lovely.

"I, uh, my face…" Hell, she had no idea how to tell him what she looked like.

"I know, Becky. We talked to the cab driver and he said you'd been beaten up. It's okay. It'll all be okay."

Becky nodded, knowing Dean couldn't see her. Thank goodness he already knew about her face. She figured he knew on one hand, but seeing it would be another story. Oh, well. Nothing she could do about that now.

Becky and Dean continued to talk about nothing in particular until Dean finally told her they were pulling up into the hospital parking lot and he'd be with her soon. They finally hung up. Becky sat on the edge of the bed nervously. They hadn't admitted her. She was beaten up, but as she'd told Steve, she was essentially all right. They'd put her right arm into a sling to keep her immobile so her collarbone could heal.

She was sitting on the edge of the bed, wearing the stupid hospital gown that was way too short when Dean, his parents and Jonathan came through the curtain. She looked up nervously. She had no time to say anything before Dean had caught her up in his arms and was holding her tightly.

Becky's face was nestled up against his throat. Her one good arm went around his waist without thought, while the other was smushed again his chest, secure in its sling. She felt one of his hands at the back of her head, holding her head to him gently, and the other was against her back, holding her close. She lost it. She couldn't stop the tears to save her life. Dean was here. He'd make everything better.

Dean turned them around and sat on the edge of the bed, holding Becky to him. God. He'd only gotten a glimpse of her face but that one glimpse was bad enough. He'd seen women who'd been beaten up before, but not someone who belonged to him. Not someone in *his* family. Not someone he loved. He suddenly knew how the relatives of the women he'd helped felt. Helpless. Like riding in a train car with no breaks. There was nothing you could do to make the hurt go away. The only thing he could do was hold her and let her cry. He was shaking. Him. The rock. Shaking. His *One* was hurt and he'd never let her go again.

Dean didn't know how long he'd been sitting on the bed holding Becky, but when he finally lifted his head and looked around he saw that his family was no longer in the room. They'd given him the privacy he needed with his woman.

Becky had stopped crying a bit ago and was now just sniffling. He could feel the wetness on his neck from her tears. He looked down at Becky and said, trying to lighten the moment, "You aren't wiping your snot on me, are you?"

Becky laughed lightly as he wanted her to. He took the hand that had been on her head and put a finger under her chin, raising her head until he could see her face fully for the first time. He held back his gasp and tried to look at her objectively.

She had two black eyes, and dark circles under them. Her lip was cut and had obviously been stitched, probably just that morning. He ran his thumb lightly over her lips while continuing to run his gaze over her face. God, what had she been through? And by who? He needed to hear the story, but he'd wait until she was ready. It was enough, for now, she was here in his arms and in one piece.

"Can you tell me what happened now, sweetheart? If not, that's okay, I'll wait, but please know you can trust me. I'm here for you. Nothing you say will change the feelings I have for you."

He watched as Becky nodded and quietly gathered her thoughts.

"I've watched TV, I've seen movies, I've read stories…" she began softly, "but I never thought I'd be in the position to be scared for my life and wonder if I'd live to see the next day."

Dean's arms tightened, and he consciously had to tell himself to loosen his hold. This was going to be torture for him, but he knew Becky had to get it out. Hell, he had to hear it. He wanted to know everything she went through so he could best figure out how to help her.

Becky continued, understanding that Dean had himself under control and he'd let her tell the story her way.

"I never figured anyone would hate me enough to want to hurt me. I couldn't understand that kind of hate. But I get it now. It's irrational. I tried to stop it, but eventually I figured out that they weren't going to stop no matter what I said."

"They?" Dean interrupted, barely holding on to his anger.

Becky nodded, and ignoring Dean's interruption continued. She told Dean everything that had happened after he'd left for the mountains. How she'd had enough after Derek had tried to attack her after their date.

Afraid Dean would lose control she was surprised when he simply said, "Good for you, Becky. You knew it was time to get out and you did."

"I wasn't scared at all when I left the house. All I could think of was you, and how I'd finally get to be with you out in public. It was such a relief." She sighed. She told Dean about seeing Derek and David getting out of the limo and having a bad feeling about it. She told him about how stupid she'd been by deciding to eat in the restaurant when she should've been staying in her room avoiding all the former contestants. She explained how the twins intercepted her while she was eating and about how drunk they were. She even told him about the attempted rapes and when they couldn't get hard how they'd started taunting her and hitting her. It wasn't until she started telling him about them writing on her that she broke down again.

"You know, as I lay on the floor of that hotel room I convinced myself it was better for them to hit me than to rape me. They hadn't broken me. I could take that. It wasn't until they got out the markers and started writing on me that I lost it."

Becky started to shake uncontrollably and Dean had

to lean down so his ear was right next to her mouth to hear her next words. "I couldn't stand it that others would see what they did. It was one thing for them to try to rape me, no one could see that, no one would know, but to write all over me was different. Everyone would see. I couldn't go to your dad, Dean," she said miserably, "he'd *see* what they did."

"Ah Jesus, sweetheart," Dean crooned to the devastated woman in his arms. How did he make her understand what Derek and David did to her wasn't what people would see?

"My family sees *you*, Becky. What they did to you, isn't *you*. *You* are the woman their son is in love with. *You* are the woman who came to that refuge center and sat down on the ground and did whatever you could to make a small defenseless animal feel comfortable. *You* are mine, Becky. Mine. That's what they would've seen."

He let her cry against him again. God. If only her tears could wash away the feeling of those men touching her. If only they could wash away the feelings of helplessness and humiliation she was feeling.

Finally, Becky pulled back again and shyly looked up at Dean.

"You're in love with me?"

"God, yes. I know we have a long road ahead of us. You have to get some help too, so you can deal with what happened. We need to get you moved down here. We need to spend time together, just the two of us, and really get to know each other. But ultimately, I know deep in my heart, you're mine. You belong to me and I belong to you. I hope to Christ you'll learn to feel the same way, but I want you to know up front where I'm coming from. I'm not leaving you. I'll be at your side as we deal with this together."

"I want that too," she said, looking into his eyes.

She leaned forward and placed her lips lightly on his. Dean didn't want to hurt her and he gently ran his tongue along the seam of her lips, avoiding her stiches, and then pulled back.

"What did the doctor say? Are you allowed to leave?"

"I think she wants to come back in and talk to me some more. I already talked to the police…they took pictures," her voice cracked, but she bravely continued, "and said they'd be in touch."

Dean nodded. "Okay, we'll deal with them when they get back in touch with you. Are you allowed to get dressed?"

Becky nodded. "Are you going to help me?"

Dean shook his head. At seeing the shock and hurt in Becky's eyes at his negative answer, he quickly said, "The marker and the words don't matter one whit to me, sweetheart. Don't get me wrong, I want to literally kill them for hurting you, for doing that to you. But don't think for one second I don't want to look at your gorgeous body. I want to spend hours examining you and making sure you're all right. I want to take my time and check out all the nooks and crannies of what makes you, you. I want to lay you down and make love to you for hours and worship your body, *but* I want it to be at a time that *we* decide. In our bed. I want the first time I see you to be special for us both. I don't want it to be in a hospital room wondering if someone is going to walk in. I'll see what those assholes did to you Becky, make no mistake, but now isn't the time. Okay?"

Becky could only nod. God, every time he opened his mouth he slayed her with his sincerity and emotion.

"I'll just go and get my family while you get dressed. I'll send in a nurse to help you navigate around that sling. We'll meet you back here to talk with the doctor and I'll take you home."

Becky slowly got dressed with the nurse's help, thinking about all that had happened to her in the last couple of days. She'd had such extreme highs and lows she was amazed she was still standing upright. One thing was clear, however, Dean wanted her. She smiled and waited for him to return for her.

Dean returned and Steve, Bethany and Jonathan crowded into the small room behind him. Each of them gave her a huge gentle hug and didn't demand answers, she was thankful they were tactful enough to give her some time.

Finally, the doctor came in to talk to all of them.

"You're Rebecca's family?" she asked with a raised eyebrow.

Dean answered for all of them, "Yes, I'm her fiancé, and these are her future father and mother-in-law and brother-in-law."

The doctor looked to Becky for confirmation and she could only nod. She shouldn't have been shocked by Dean's words, but deep down she still was. She hadn't been a hundred percent sure he was serious about the entire being together thing, but obviously he was.

Dr. Sumner ran down the list of injuries Becky had. When she was done, Becky could see Dean and his family were looking a bit queasy.

"Honestly, guys," she said, trying to make them feel better. "It sounds a lot worse than it is."

"No, Becky," Jonathan disagreed, "it sounds just as bad as it looks. You're coming home with us, aren't you? You'll let us take care of you while you heal?"

Dean answered for her, "Yes, she's coming with me."

The others just nodded their heads as if it was a foregone conclusion all along.

Dr. Sumner wrote out a couple of prescriptions. One for pain and one for antibiotics. She encouraged

Becky to go to her own physician for a follow-up in a few days. Becky was about to explain that she wasn't from around here and didn't have a doctor when Bethany piped up.

"Becky, I have a great physician. I'll make you an appointment. If you like her, then you can set up further visits with her."

It was settled. Becky was on her way home with Dean and his family. There was no place she'd rather be.

## Chapter Fifteen

✦

BECKY KNEW THE time had arrived to talk to Dean's family. They'd been so great to her. Very patient, and they didn't ask her why she hadn't come to them or anything. She owed them an explanation, but she only wanted to do it once. She didn't think she had the strength to go over it more than one time.

When they arrived back at the refuge center, which was also Steve and Bethany's home, they settled her on the couch and ran around trying to get her everything they thought she needed to be comfortable. Bethany brought her a pillow and a soft fleece blanket. Steve brought her a large class of water and Jonathan hovered nearby as if waiting for her to ask about needing something. Dean sat next to her on the couch and held her hand, not saying a word, but providing some much needed support just by being there.

"I wanted to talk to you all if you'd let me," Becky told them with only a hint of emotion making her voice crack. "I want to explain what I was thinking and why I didn't immediately come to you."

"Oh, honey," Bethany said immediately. "We understand."

"No," Becky said quickly. "You don't, but I'm hoping you will after I'm done."

Understanding this was apparently important to her, they all sat down around the couch to hear what she had to say.

"After I left the hotel I didn't know what to do. All sorts of thoughts were racing through my head. I thought I could just leave and pretend that nothing had happened. As time went on I started to hurt more and more. Everything hurt."

She could feel Dean tense beside her, but she tried to ignore it and continue.

"I got mad, at myself and at Derek and David. Who were they to do this to me and get away with it? If they'd done it to me, how many others would they do it to as well? Would they succeed in actually raping someone else? Had they done it in the past? I knew I had to stop them. But I was also mad at myself. I'm usually not so pathetic. I should've come to you guys right away. I know you would've helped me and not made me feel bad. I did know it. But I was embarrassed. I'm still embarrassed that you know what happened. I didn't want you guys to look at me with guilt or pity."

She took a deep breath. This next part was hard.

"I'm afraid you'll look at me differently now. Not just because of what my face looks like or because you know what happened to me, but because I let you all down. For all my talk about getting that little coyote to trust, at the first sign of trouble, *I* didn't trust you. I really am sorry I didn't contact you right away, Steve. I mean, I know I should have, but I was a coward."

Steve got up from his seat and came toward the vulnerable young woman sitting next to his son. He put his finger up to her lips gently to keep her from saying anything until he said his peace.

"You could never be a coward, Becky. You just needed some time to process what happened to you. In the end you *did* contact me. You called me to help you and we came. What I feel for you, what we all feel for you, isn't pity. We're sorry this happened. We're so sorry you're hurt and you had to go through that awful experience. We're pissed for you. We're pissed at those men. But there's no pity. The only thing we feel when we look at you is joy that you're here with us, with Dean, and that you'll be okay."

Becky sniffed and nodded. She leaned toward Steve hesitantly and put her one good arm around his neck. "Thank you, Steve. Thank you."

Steve hugged his son's woman gently, knowing she was still in pain. "I hope at some point you'll feel comfortable enough to call me Dad."

Becky leaned back to feel Dean's hand against her lower back. "I'd be honored…Dad," she said softly and grinned lopsidedly at him.

Becky turned when Dean said, "I'm just so sorry I wasn't there to protect you, sweetheart. That this had to happen to you…"

Becky shook her head. "It's not your fault, Dean. It would've happened if you'd been in town or not."

Dean shook his head, knowing that wasn't true. "We're going to have to disagree on that one, sweetheart. If I was in town, the second you left that damn show I would've picked up you and brought you home."

"But the contract…" Becky started to say.

"The hell with the contract. I would've brought you to my home, where you would've been safe," he told her, running his hand over her head and cupping her cheek again.

Becky closed her eyes and leaned against his hand.

She didn't want to admit to what she'd done, but she had to get it all out now. "I screwed up," she baldly told the group around her.

At the shake of Dean's head and the frown on Steve's face, she nodded her head. "Yes, I did. I knew I waited too long to come to the hospital after it happened and I took a shower." She bowed her head. "I knew I'd be destroying evidence, but I had to…I just had to." Her voice got really soft. "I did keep my clothes separate and they took samples when I did come in…I just hope it's enough."

Bethany was the one who came over toward Becky next and she put her hand on Becky's leg. "It's okay, Becky, believe me when I say we don't blame you and I know I would've done the same thing."

Becky didn't know how she'd gotten so lucky to have met this family, but she knew she'd be thanking her lucky stars for the rest of her life. They'd been so supportive and she knew she'd be a mess if it wasn't for them.

"Okay, guys," Bethany said a bit more cheerily, trying to lighten the mood a bit. "Let's go. Becky needs her rest. Dean, you stay."

Dean managed a smile. He loved his mom. She always seemed to know what someone needed, and right now Becky needed some time to process all his family had said and done for her.

Bethany and Steve left the room, but before Jonathan left, he came up to the couch and touched Becky on the shoulder.

"I'll take care of this for you," he said quietly. "I'm so sorry I wasn't there for you. I knew something was wrong and I came to the hotel that night, but when I couldn't find you I left. I shouldn't have, and for that I'll never forgive myself."

He turned to leave, but Becky reached up and

grabbed his hand.

"Jonathan…please…this isn't your fault. Please, look at me," Becky pleaded with him.

Jonathan looked into her eyes and Becky could see how much he was torturing himself over her. She reached up and placed her hand on the side of his face, amazed at how right it felt and how she wasn't scared, even though this was the first time she'd ever touched this man. She was half afraid she'd never be normal again and never be able to touch another man without having flashbacks.

"Thank you for looking for me," she told him quietly. "I know you would've done everything you could to help me if you could have, and I'll forever be grateful for that." And amazingly she *did* know it. She wasn't sure if it was because of the odd connection she had with Dean or what, but she knew Jonathan would've done anything he could have for her.

Jonathan nodded. "Thanks, Becky. I'm going to go to the police station and talk to them about what I know about those two. I've watched them for the last month or so through the camera lens and I think I could probably help with some more information. I'm also going to talk to the other camera operators to see if they'd also help."

At seeing Becky's face drain of color, he quickly reassured her. "They don't know all that happened,

Becky. All they know is that Derek and David beat you up. They don't know about…anything else."

Becky nodded and tried to remind herself she didn't do anything wrong. "Okay, any help they can give to get those two off the streets is good. I appreciate your help, Jonathan."

He leaned down and kissed her on the cheek, squeezed her hand and left the room.

Becky leaned back carefully so her back was to Dean's chest. He turned them so they were reclining on the couch. Dean put his arm around Becky's waist and held her to him. He couldn't believe he could've lost her. If Derek and David had been a bit more sober, or even had gotten their hands on some sort of weapon, they easily could've killed her. He'd seen it happen too many times in his line of work to take for granted the close call his *One* had.

He kissed the top of her head. "Relax, sweetheart. I've got you. We'll get this all figured out…later. For now, just relax and know you're safe. I'll always keep you safe."

Becky nodded off to sleep, secure in the knowledge that she was safe in Dean's arms.

## Epilogue

✦

THE LAST COUPLE of months had gone by in a blur for Becky. She'd stayed with Dean's family until she'd been able to move without pain and Dean had quickly moved her into his home. It was, of course, gorgeous. She ended up quitting her underwriting job because Dean's parents had offered her the chance to work at the refuge center with them. They'd sworn it wasn't a pity job, and Becky eventually believed them. She worked her butt off and loved every minute.

Dean agreed to move Star into their home. It was a bit of a risk, since she wasn't a full blooded domestic dog, but Star had proven to be very loyal to Becky and hardly ever left her side. She was allowed to come to the refuge center every day with Becky and seemed to know when it was appropriate to laze around on the porch at the house when she was working with skittish abused animals, and when it was okay to tag along aside her as she did chores. Even when it looked like Star was sound asleep on the porch, she always knew where Becky was.

It was as if the two of them had some telepathic connection with each other. The second Becky would finish working with an animal Star couldn't be around, the little coyote-mix would bound off the porch and find her beloved Becky.

Dean told Becky about how Star had kept the scrap of fabric she'd torn off her sleeve when Becky came to say goodbye. Becky was amazed. All she could do was hug the little coyote-mix and thank her for her unconditional love.

Derek and David had been found. Incredibly, they hadn't even been hiding. Jonathan had kept his word and gone to the police, along with Kina and a few other camera operators and they'd told the cops everything they knew about the brothers. It turned out they'd actually been arrested in the past for attempted rape, but because the woman was scared to testify, they hadn't been convicted of the crime.

Derek had tried to claim the night was consensual, and David had tried to blame everything on his brother. So much for brotherly love. They were eventually sentenced to five years in jail for kidnapping and attempted rape, among other things. They were convicted mostly based on the testimony from Becky. She knew they probably wouldn't spend that much time in jail and would make probation, but she was glad at least they'd pay for what they did to her. She didn't worry about them coming after her, she had Dean, and Jonathan, and their parents and all of the employees who worked at the refuge looking out for her. She felt safe.

Becky hadn't wanted to testify. It scared her to death to face the two men in the courtroom, but she knew she had to. She knew they'd do it to someone else eventually if she chickened out. With the help of her therapist, and her new family, she was able to get through the trial.

Dean and his family had been amazing. She knew her own family had loved her, but the no strings attached love Steve and Bethany had shown her was amazing. They joked with her, and even sometimes cried with her when she needed it. Amazingly, it didn't even feel awkward.

Becky couldn't believe how much she loved Dean. When he'd taken her home after she got out of the hospital he'd done exactly what he said he would. He undressed her slowly and lovingly caressed every inch of her body. The words Derek and David had written on her body in the permanent marker were still faintly visible and he'd kissed every single one and replaced the memory of them being etched on her body with the memory of his lips kissing and nipping at her skin. He never took his own clothes off that first night, not wanting her to feel any pressure or remember how *their* naked bodies felt against her own. After trying to wipe out all the negative emotions she'd received at their hands, he simply wrapped her up in his arms and held her all night long.

Dean never told her he hadn't slept at all that night, but she'd overheard him telling Jonathan. Apparently, he'd watched her sleep and cried. He was just so overcome with emotions. He'd finally gotten to see firsthand what those two creeps had done to her body. It was such a bittersweet moment. He told Jonathan he'd been overwhelmed with joy at being able to touch her for the first time, but also furious at how she'd been violated. She never told him she'd overheard him having the emotional conversation with his brother, but hearing his words helped her heal. He hadn't been disgusted at seeing her. Rather more awestruck at how strong she'd been to get through it.

It took some time for Becky to convince herself she'd done all she could to get away and to let go of the negative feelings that had lingered. The weekly visits to the therapist helped immensely. Every now and then when she felt overwhelmed she'd make an appointment to go back and see her. Every time, she felt lighter. She knew eventually she wouldn't need to see her anymore, but for now she was content.

One night while they were eating dinner at the refuge, Steve told Becky the story about the men in their family and their *One*. She was amazed.

"Was that how it happened with you?" she'd asked Dean incredulously. He'd only nodded and said calmly, "Yes, I knew you belonged to me from the moment I saw you look up from that rock at Devil's Canyon and your eyes met mine."

Becky knew she was the luckiest woman alive. And to think if it hadn't been for the stupid reality show she never would've met Dean.

Jonathan was currently in Alaska on his last assignment as a camera operator. He hadn't wanted to go, but Becky convinced him she was fine. She knew he still felt guilty about not searching harder for her when he'd gone to the hotel that night, but she'd tried to reassure him that there wasn't anything else he could've done.

Jonathan was excited to move back to Arizona to be with his family and start working with Dean. He'd seen firsthand how abusive people could be and he wanted to be a part of protecting those who needed it.

Eddie and his production crew got off relatively easily after the fiasco with Derek and David. The lawyers tried to convince Becky to press charges against Eddie on the grounds he should've done a more extensive background check on the applicants for the show. They argued if he had, then Derek and David's past allegations against them would've come to light and Becky never would've been hurt. Becky declined. She honestly just didn't want to think about it anymore and wanted to put the entire nightmare behind her.

Dean gave her the best advice, though. Becky still grinned every time she thought about it. He suggested the lawyers get in writing as a part of the condition of her not suing Eddie and the production company in the future, that the reality show never be aired. Becky didn't think Eddie would go for it, especially considering how much money had already been spent on the production of the show, but surprisingly he did. She supposed he probably had some pressure put on him from the executives, but whatever the reason, she was thrilled.

Becky didn't have to worry about what she'd look like to millions of people and she *never* had to worry about seeing re-runs of Derek and David haunting her forever. She thought about Marissa and how all her dreams of becoming famous went down the drain and had to laugh. Becky figured she deserved it. She felt bad for about ten minutes, but Dean distracted her by picking her up and carrying her to their bedroom, and all thoughts of Marissa and what she thought disappeared in an instant.

✷

JONATHAN STOOD IN the wind and shivered. God, he couldn't wait to be done with this stupid show and get back to Arizona where it was warm. He looked out of the corner of his eye at Kina. Kina. His *One*. She was standing next to him, also filming. He'd been blown away when he'd gone to talk to her after they'd found Becky and realized in an instant that Kina was his. Damn. He hadn't ever really talked to her much or even seen her very often on the set in Arizona. It was only when he needed her help he'd actually realized that not only was she incredibly beautiful, but she was the one woman made especially for him.

He never really believed the *One* nonsense his dad had always talked about growing up, until he'd seen it happen to his brother. Dean had taken one look at Becky and known he wanted to spend the rest of his life with her. It'd taken a while, but eventually Becky fell for him too and now, even after everything Becky had gone through, they were together and happy.

Jonathan knew Kina would be a different story. She was hard. He didn't know how he knew that, but he did. She didn't smile much and he'd overheard her talking with another camera operator about how she didn't believe in love anymore. Something had happened to her to make her think that way. He was trying to figure out a way to get closer to her, but it was difficult. She stayed to herself and didn't encourage the other camera operators to get close to her. He'd find a way, though, he had to. She was his. Even if she didn't know it. She'd figure it out in the long run.

# Discover other titles by Susan Stoker

## Beyond Reality Series
*Outback Hearts*
*Flaming Hearts*
*Frozen Hearts*

## Badge of Honor: Texas Heroes Series
*Justice for Mackenzie*
*Justice for Mickie*
*Justice for Corrie*
*Justice for Laine (novella)*
*Shelter for Elizabeth*
*Justice for Boone*
*Shelter for Adeline (TBA)*
*Justice for Sidney (TBA)*
*Shelter for Blythe (TBA)*
*Justice for Milena (TBA)*
*Shelter for Sophie (TBA)*
*Justice for Kinley (TBA)*
*Shelter for Promise (TBA)*
*Shelter for Koren (TBA)*
*Shelter for Penelope (TBA)*

**Delta Force Heroes Series**
*Rescuing Rayne*
*Assisting Aimee (loosely related to DF)*
*Rescuing Emily*
*Rescuing Harley*
*Rescuing Kassie (TBA)*
*Rescuing Casey (TBA)*
*Rescuing Wendy (TBA)*
*Rescuing Mary (TBA)*

**SEAL of Protection Series**
*Protecting Caroline*
*Protecting Alabama*
*Protecting Fiona*
*Marrying Caroline (novella)*
*Protecting Summer*
*Protecting Cheyenne*
*Protecting Jessyka*
*Protecting Julie (novella)*
*Protecting Melody*
*Protecting the Future*

**Writing as Annie George**
*Stepbrother Virgin (erotic novella)*

# Connect with Susan Online

**_Susan's Facebook Profile and Page:_**
www.facebook.com/authorsstoker
www.facebook.com/authorsusanstoker

**_Follow Susan on Twitter:_**
www.twitter.com/Susan_Stoker

**_Find Susan's Books on Goodreads:_**
www.goodreads.com/SusanStoker

**_Email:_** Susan@StokerAces.com

**_Website:_** www.StokerAces.com

**_To sign up for Susan's Newsletter go to:_**
http://bit.ly/SusanStokerNewsletter

**_Or text:_** STOKER to 24587 for text alerts on your mobile device

# About the Author

*New York Times*, *USA Today,* and *Wall Street Journal* Bestselling Author Susan Stoker has a heart as big as the state of Texas, where she lives, but this all-American girl has also spent the last fourteen years living in Missouri, California, Colorado, and Indiana. She's married to a retired Army man who now gets to follow *her* around the country.

She debuted her first series in 2014 and quickly followed that up with the SEAL of Protection Series, which solidified her love of writing and creating stories readers can get lost in.

If you enjoyed this book, or any book, please consider leaving a review. It's appreciated by authors more than you'll know.

Printed in Great Britain
by Amazon